Lincoln Public Library

December 1974

The Innocents

The Innocents

GEORGES SIMENON

Translated from the French by Eileen Ellenbogen

A HELEN AND KURT WOLFF BOOK

HARCOURT BRACE JOVANOVICH, INC., NEW YORK

December 1974

Printed in the United States of America

Library of Congress Cataloging in Publication Data

Simenon, Georges, 1903–
The innocents.

"A Helen and Kurt Wolff book."
I. Title.
PZ3.S5892In [PQ2637.I53]   843'.9'12   73–16004
ISBN 0–15–144430–7

First American edition

B C D E

The Innocents

1

Even the March rain, which had been coming down for the past hour, was something to be relished. It made the colors in the workshop seem softer, more intimate. The roofs of Paris, varnished by the rain, were black with a bluish tinge, and the sky a faintly luminous gray.

Célerin, more familiarly known to his assistants as Monsieur Georges, was standing at his drawing board filling in the details of a working sketch for a brooch that had long been taking shape in his mind, inspired by a painting he had seen in the window of a picture gallery. It was a thistle in three shades of gold.

He was never without a cigarette and, as usual, it had gone out and was stuck to his lower lip. As he worked, he hummed a bar or two of an old song—all he could remember of it.

Jules Daven, the oldest of his assistants, was bent over his workbench, which was covered with precision tools so tiny that they seemed fit only for children to play with: gravers, needle files, pliers, burnishers, drills, drawplates, saw blades and T squares.

In his hand was a blowpipe, the flame of which was reduced to little more than a bluish thread.

His friend Létang, who at forty-nine had seven chil-

3

dren and whose wife was expecting her eighth, was shaving a bar of gold into thin sheets.

Pierrot, the most recent addition to the team, had just finished setting a stone in a ring, and was now polishing it.

The glass door was closed, indicating that Madame Coutance, who was in charge of the shop, was attending to a customer.

"Shop" was perhaps not quite the right word for it, since it was situated on the top floor of an old building on Rue de Sévigné that had once been a private house.

It was, nonetheless, fitted out like a shop, with a long waxed pine counter, and showcases all round the walls in which the jewelry was displayed.

Célerin felt happy, at peace with himself and with the world.

For ten years he had been an employee of a large firm of jewelers on Rue Saint-Honoré. Then another employee of the firm, a salesman called Brassier, had come into a sizable inheritance, and had offered to set the two of them up in business on their own.

Naturally Brassier, having provided the capital, was the senior partner, but the arrangement had worked smoothly for sixteen years.

Brassier was seldom to be found on the premises in the Rue de Sévigné. It was he who made the rounds of the leading jewelers, showing samples and taking orders. The workshop was Célerin's own little kingdom.

The atmosphere was informal, and they often sent young Pierrot out to get a bottle of Beaujolais from a bistro nearby.

As to Daven, the senior assistant, although well on in his fifties, he was the resident comic, with a seemingly endless flow of entertaining stories.

Can any man call himself happy? Célerin believed

that he was, and that nothing could rob him of his happiness. He loved his work. He was his own master. As to his wife and children, he had no worries on their account.

He was in the prime of life. His health had always been good, and had not deteriorated with the passing of time.

Voices, a little raised, could be heard in the shop; then the sound of the outer door opening. This, however, was not the end. Conversation between a high pitched voice and another, more muted—that of Madame Coutance—continued in the doorway.

"I bet you anything you like it's Old Mother Papin," grumbled Daven.

This was the widow Papin, or Madame Veuve Papin, as she liked to call herself.

She was a very rich woman and one of their best customers, but she was also a pain in the neck.

At last they heard the outer door shut. The communicating glass door between the workroom and the shop opened to admit Madame Coutance in a state of exhaustion.

"Old Mother Papin," she murmured, by way of explanation. Daven had been right.

Madame Coutance was approaching forty. Her husband had died very young. She was plump, with a rather chubby face, and she was always smiling.

"This time, it's about a cameo . . ." She handed it to Célerin, who examined it carefully.

"It's a superb piece—Empire, I should think. From the quality of the workmanship, I'd say it was done by one of the finest craftsmen of the day. It might even be a portrait of the Empress Josephine. . . . What does she want?"

"She wants it reset."

5

"But it's a period setting, which greatly enhances the value of the cameo."

"So I tried to tell her, but you know what she's like. 'I'm fed up with all that old-fashioned stuff.'"

Rich in her own right, she had also inherited jewelry from an aunt who had amassed a great deal in the course of a long life.

She was now in the process of having it brought up to date. Up to date, as far as she was concerned, meant in the style of about 1900. She spent hours over each piece, arguing about it in her high-pitched voice. Her face was mauve—she used a peculiar shade of powder —and she always wore a hat trimmed with sequins.

Her name—there was no getting away from it—was Papin, since she had married Papin, the ball-bearings tycoon; but she had been born Hélène de Molincourt, and she never allowed anyone to forget it, any more than she allowed anyone to forget that her status was that of widow.

On her visiting cards and stationery, her name appeared as "Papin, *née* de Molincourt."

From her aged aunt, she had also inherited a château of that name in the Cher region.

Daven mimicked her mannerisms to perfection. He could even imitate her distinctive, high-pitched voice. He put the cameo down on his bench. There was no safe —bars of gold and platinum, precious and semiprecious stones were left lying about on shelves—and, in all the years, nothing had ever been lost.

The shop-door buzzer sounded. There was an enamel plate above the bell push that read: "Do not ring. Enter." From where he was standing, Célerin was the first to catch sight of a flat police cap, and presumed that he was going to be told to move his car yet again.

The policeman gave a little cough, and looked about him inquiringly. Then, as he walked toward the workshop door, Célerin came forward to meet him.

"Is Monsieur Célerin here? Georges Célerin?"

"I'm Célerin . . . What's the trouble? My car again?"

"No, sir. I'm not a traffic officer, and this is not, in fact, my area. I am Sergeant Fernaud of the Eighth Arrondissement . . ."

He seemed embarrassed, and looked around the workshop in some surprise. He had evidently never seen anything like it before.

"Could we go into your office?"

"I have no office. You may speak freely in front of my colleagues. What's all this about?"

The sergeant touched his cap.

"I'm sorry, Monsieur Célerin, I have bad news for you. You are, are you not, the husband of Annette-Marie Stéphanie Célerin?"

"That is my wife's name, yes."

"She has met with an accident."

"What sort of an accident?"

"She was run over by a truck on Rue Washington."

"Are you sure there hasn't been some mistake? I don't see how my wife could have been anywhere near the Champs-Élysées. She's a social worker and her area is Saint-Antoine . . . Saint-Paul . . ."

"All the same, the accident occurred on Rue Washington."

"Is it serious?"

Almost in a whisper, Sergeant Fernaud murmured:

"She was dead on arrival at the hospital—the Lariboisière."

"Annette? Dead?"

7

The others stared at him blankly. It was so sudden, so utterly unforeseen, that they simply could not believe it.

"I want to see her."

"We naturally waited to get in touch with you before removing the body to the Forensic Laboratory."

Célerin changed out of his long white working overalls and put on the jacket of his suit. He was dry-eyed. His face was set, as though he were beyond any expression of grief.

As he was going out the door he turned back and said, conscious of how absurd it must sound:

"Sorry about this."

There was no elevator. They walked down the four flights of stairs, Célerin ahead.

"Wouldn't it be better if I came with you?"

"Perhaps. I'd feel lost in a hospital. We've never had any serious illness in the family."

"Do you have children?"

"Two. How did you know where to find me?"

"We got the address on Boulevard Beaumarchais from your wife's identity card. . . . I presume that is where you live?"

"Yes."

"A very nice lady with a foreign accent answered the door. I asked her where I could get in touch with you, and she gave me this address on Rue de Sévigné."

"Did you tell her what it was about?"

"No . . . Do you have a car?"

A small white Citroen was parked on the other side of the street. They both got in. It was still raining. Somehow, in March the rain seemed more penetrating than at other times of the year, but it did not screen out the light to the same extent.

"How did it happen?"

The sergeant looked at him with a touch of awe, as though, because of his misfortune, Célerin was set apart from other men and somehow larger than life.

"I don't know the precise details. Inquiries are still in progress at the scene of the accident. All I do know is that it happened just opposite a greengrocer's shop, Manotti's. We have a statement from a man who was passing at the time . . . You have to go in the direction of the Gare du Nord. The Lariboisière Hospital is on Rue Ambroise-Paré."

"Was my wife crossing the road?"

"Apparently, according to two witnesses, she had just come out of a nearby house—there's some conflict of evidence as to which house it was . . . She seemed to be in a hurry. She was walking very fast, almost running. Then she stepped onto the road, intending to cross over. It was slippery underfoot on account of the rain . . . She slipped and fell in front of a delivery van, too late for the driver to stop. She was crushed under the wheels. . . .

"Our man at once called a doctor and an ambulance. Although her ribs were crushed, she was still breathing . . ."

"Was she able to speak?"

"No. Forgive me for telling you this, but she was bringing up a lot of blood. There was a doctor in the ambulance, Doctor Vigier. He took charge of her at once.

"Our man on the spot rang Divisional Headquarters. Two men went straight to Rue Washington, and I went to the hospital."

"Did you see her?"

"Yes."

"Where was she?"

"All the beds in Casualty were full. They had to

9

leave her in the corridor, along with three or four other accident cases. Doctor Vigier was still with her.

" 'Here's her identity card,' he said. 'You'll be wanting to go to her home address and inform her next of kin.' "

"How did she look?"

"She was covered with a sheet. I just lifted it a little."

"No. I don't want to hear . . ."

Strangely enough, he was very calm, as though all feeling had been frozen out of him. He threaded his way through the traffic and drew up at the front entrance of the Lariboisière Hospital.

"The next entrance. Casualty."

The ground-floor corridor was tiled all over in yellow. A young doctor was bending over an old man who lay staring at the ceiling, an empty stare, the eyes already glazing over. There were two other beds, each covered in a sheet.

"I'll go and get Doctor Vigier."

Célerin, in a daze, stood where he was. The nurse on duty pointed to a chair, and suggested that he should sit down.

He must have thanked her mechanically.

But he was not sure. Everything about him was tilting and swaying. The walls, the floor, the people seemed insubstantial. He looked around, feeling remote, indifferent.

The young doctor came toward him from the far end of the long corridor and held out his hand:

"Monsieur Célerin?"

"Yes."

"I'm Doctor Vigier. I attended your wife on the way here from Rue Washington, but I could see at once, unfortunately, that it was too late. In a way, you might look on it as a happy release. I'm sure you wouldn't wish me to go into the medical details . . . Suffice it to say that her lungs and abdomen were crushed and perforated . . ."

"Can I see her?"

The doctor folded the sheet back, exposing her face. They must have washed her, since there was no trace of blood to be seen. She looked astonishingly peaceful.

First he touched her cheek with two fingers, as though he meant to stroke it, then he bent and put his lips to her white forehead.

Vigier murmured:

"They'll be here shortly to take her to the Forensic Laboratory. There will have to be an autopsy, I imagine."

"Why?"

"With insurance, one can never tell . . . I'll give you her handbag. I took the liberty of opening it, just to take a look at her identity card for her address. Have you been married long?"

"Twenty years . . . We were going to celebrate our twentieth wedding anniversary next month."

"Do you have children?"

"Two."

"Are they old enough to be understanding?"

"I don't know. The elder, the boy, is sixteen, and my daughter is fourteen and a half."

The mortuary van from the Forensic Laboratory drew up at the entrance. Two men got out and came toward them carrying a stretcher.

"Which shall we take first?" asked one of the men, pointing to the beds.

Célerin, standing to one side, asked nervously:

"What should I do now?"

"The best thing would be for you to go home and

11

break the news to your children. . . . The body will be returned to you in a day or two."

"Thank you."

He did not know whether he ought to shake hands or not. He no longer knew anything. He saw, to his surprise, that the sergeant was still there, waiting for him.

"Will you be all right on your own?"

"Why not?"

What an extraordinary thing to ask, he thought. He felt utterly lost. First there was that shower of luminous rain striking the cobblestones. Then Old Mother Papin and her cameo, which she wanted reset in Edwardian style. And finally the flat police cap . . .

Annette was dead. They had taken her to what used to be called the morgue. In a daze, he shook hands with the sergeant and stopped himself just in time from driving off in the wrong direction. It was nearly six o'clock. The traffic was heavy, with cars almost bumper to bumper.

He had been on the point of going back to Rue de Sévigné; he could not have said why. There he would have been among friends. He would have been back in the surroundings in which he felt most at home, and there perhaps he might have been able gradually to reestablish contact with the world of everyday reality.

Annette had no business to be on Rue Washington. The aged, the sick, the destitute whom she visited all lived in a compact area between Rue Saint-Paul and the Bastille. That was why she had not needed a car.

His son, Jean-Jacques, and his daughter, Marlène, must have been back from school for some time by now, and they still knew nothing of what had happened. Even if Nathalie had mentioned the police sergeant's visit, they would have assumed that it had to do with a parking offense.

Nothing dramatic had ever happened to them as a family. Nothing. Not so much as a serious quarrel.

He parked his car, as usual, on Boulevard Beaumarchais; then, as he was walking past a bistro—he had been there a couple of times in the past—he stopped, hesitated, and finally went in. He made straight for the bar and, with a feeling of shame, ordered a brandy.

The proprietor, who knew him by sight, was puzzled by his appearance.

"Is there anything wrong, Monsieur Célerin?"

He hesitated, stared at the man whom he knew to be called Léon, emptied his glass in a single gulp, and said tonelessly:

"My wife is dead."

"I'd never have thought she had anything wrong with her . . . And she was still a young woman . . ."

"She was killed in an accident!" he burst out almost aggressively. "Give me another!"

He drank three glasses in quick succession. Léon watched him with consternation, but also a touch of awe. His bereavement had raised his stature in the eyes of the bartender.

"Do your children know?"

"Not yet . . . I'm about to tell them."

Feeling limp, he walked home unsteadily. He went past the concierge's lodge, forgetting to stop and wave to her as he normally did. He got into the elevator and pressed the third-floor button.

It was Nathalie who opened the door. She was more than just a housekeeper. She was approaching sixty, and had been with them for eighteen years. She was a bit on the heavy side, with a plump, smiling face.

As soon as she set eyes on Célerin, she knew that something was seriously wrong.

"Did the police officer call to see you?"

"Yes."

"Well?"

"She's dead . . ."

"Dead?"

She put her hand to her mouth to stop herself from crying out.

"Madame? . . ."

"Yes."

"But how?"

"She was run over."

"In the street? Just like that?"

"That's the way it looks."

"Where is she? Will they be bringing her back here?"

"She's at the Forensic Laboratory. There will have to be an autopsy."

"Why?"

"I don't know . . . I don't know anything. . . . Where are the children?"

He felt the need for another drink. He went into the dining room, where they always kept a few bottles in the sideboard.

"Do you think you should?" Nathalie called out from behind him.

"Yes."

Had he not just lost his wife, and, because of it, was not his own life over too? If anyone had a right to a drink, surely he had. He got out a glass, larger than those provided in Léon's bistro, and filled it. He was feeling a little giddy

Someone came into the dining room. It was his son, Jean-Jacques, who started in surprise at seeing his father with a bottle in front of him and a glass of brandy in his hand.

"Go and get your sister, son."

The boy ran out and got her. Disconcerted, she stood hesitating in the doorway.

"What's the matter? You're home early . . ."

"I have bad news for you, my dears. Bad for me. Bad for everyone. Your mother has had an accident. She was knocked down by a truck."

"Is it serious?"

"It couldn't be worse. . . . She's dead."

And suddenly, without warning, he burst into tears.

Marlène cried out, and flung herself against the wall, where she stood beating it with her fists Between sobs, she gasped:

"It isn't true . . . it can't be . . . not Mother!"

As for Jean-Jacques, he was trying to control himself; as though he were already a grown man of mature understanding, he went over to his father, who had buried his face in his hands, and touched him on the shoulder.

"Don't make yourself ill, Father."

The children never called their parents Dad and Mom, but always Father and Mother—not because of any lack of feeling, but rather because their intimacy was tempered with a touch of reserve.

Scarcely realizing what he was doing, Célerin reached out for the bottle. Without a hint of reproach in his voice, Jean-Jacques murmured:

"Do you think you should?"

Célerin drew back his hand, and with a sad little smile, said gently:

"You know, son, there are worse things . . ."

"I know."

They were united by an air of gravity, abolishing, as it were, the gap of years. Marlène had taken refuge in the kitchen, most likely sobbing on Nathalie's bosom.

"It was so sudden, you see . . . so senseless . . . so pointless. If she'd been ill, one would have been prepared for it . . . And there I was, enjoying the first rain of the spring."

"What exactly happened?"

"She was hurrying along the sidewalk . . . I don't know . . . They couldn't tell me very much . . . not even what she was doing on Rue Washington. One witness says she was coming out of a house nearby . . . The road was wet . . . She was running across, and she slipped in front of a truck. The driver wasn't able to stop in time."

"How did you hear about it?"

"The police opened her bag and got this address from her identity card. A sergeant called here and found out where I worked . . ."

"And he went to the shop, I suppose, and told you there?"

"A customer had just left, Old Mother Papin . . . I've often told you about her . . . We were all laughing and joking. Then I caught sight of a policeman's cap through the door, which was open just a crack . . ."

It had stopped raining. There was even a little pallid sunshine, and the trees on Boulevard Beaumarchais were beginning to come into leaf.

They had lived in the same apartment ever since they were married.

To begin with, they had had only two rooms, with kitchen and bathroom. Luckily for them, the tenants of the neighboring apartment had retired to the country, and they were able to knock down the walls and combine the two to make quite a spacious home for themselves.

16

It was he, more than his wife, who valued comfort. It was he who liked substantial, well-polished furniture, of the kind that can still occasionally be found in small country towns. They had furnished the apartment gradually over the years, sometimes driving as much as fifty miles to attend an auction sale.

"It's too much, really, Georges."

Why too much? It was their only extravagance. They scarcely ever went out, and yet they were never bored.

The children had a bedroom each to themselves, next door to Nathalie, who, to all intents and purposes, had brought them up.

She came looking for them, red about the eyes and nose.

"Will you want dinner at the usual time?"

They normally dined at half past seven. Today, everything was out of gear. He had come home earlier than usual. On a normal day, he left the shop at seven.

"Whatever suits you, Nathalie. . . . What's Marlène doing?"

"She's gone to lie down, and I don't think she should be disturbed. It's been a great shock . . . she hasn't fully taken it in yet. It will probably be a day or two before she starts really missing her . . ."

"Should I be going to school tomorrow?" asked Jean-Jacques.

Seeing that Célerin, taken by surprise, was hesitating, Nathalie answered for him:

"And why shouldn't you?"

"I thought . . ."

For Célerin, too, a lot of things had suddenly ceased to matter. Even the children. With a sense of shame, he realized that there was no consolation for him in them.

As for the apartment . . .

17

How could he ever have attached so much importance to the furniture and knickknacks that surrounded him? They meant nothing to him any more.

There was nothing, just emptiness. He himself was empty. What were they doing to Annette at this moment? They had cut her open. No doubt there were several of them gathered around her . . . And afterward? What would happen afterward?

She would never again return to take her rightful place in her home. Never again would he hear her voice, never again hold her small, muscular hand.

He put the cork back in the bottle, ramming it down hard so as not to be tempted to take it out again. He drank very little, but all through the day and evening there was always a burned-out cigarette dangling from his lips. Today, the last he had smoked had been at the Rue de Sévigné, before leaving with the police sergeant. He lit one now, and it tasted strange to him.

"You'll have to pull yourself together, Monsieur. You can't just let yourself go, especially in front of the children."

Jean-Jacques had left the room. No doubt he, too, had taken refuge in his bedroom.

Nathalie had been born in Leningrad in the days when it was still called Saint Petersburg, a few years before the events of 1917. Her father, an officer in the guards, had been killed. Her mother and two of her aunts had suffered the same fate.

The family governess had managed to escape with the child to Constantinople, and had supported them both by giving piano lessons. Later, they had come to France and settled in Paris, and here, too, the governess had earned her living as a piano teacher.

She had also attempted to teach Nathalie, but the girl

had no ear for music; so she enrolled her in the École des beaux-arts, where she had barely scraped through the diploma course.

After the death of the governess, by which time Nathalie was a little over twenty, she worked for a while in a shop, but had difficulty in making herself understood, because of her strong foreign accent.

After that she went into service with a very rich family on Faubourg Saint-Germain that also had a château in the Nièvre and a villa on the Riviera.

In time, her employers died, and after a succession of unsatisfactory jobs, Nathalie moved in with the Célerins. She was by now more or less one of the family.

"The main thing is not to brood on it."

He stifled a nervous snigger. It was not a question of brooding. The emptiness was not only all around him, but inside him as well. He did not know what to do with himself. What was he usually doing at this time of the day? He would not yet have returned home. He would be busy in his workshop, surrounded by familiar, often smiling faces, and on the dot of seven, one or another of them would call out:

"Closing time!"

Sometimes Brassier would call in to return the pieces of jewelry that he had been showing around in the course of the day.

"The pendant is sold, and they want another three like it."

He and Brassier could not have been more different. Célerin was phlegmatic, a little on the slow side, never happier than when he was at his drawing board or his workbench.

Brassier, two years younger, was seething with ener-

19

gy, and had to be forever on the move. If he had called in at Rue de Sévigné this evening, they would surely have let him know. Or even if he had telephoned.

He slumped into his armchair facing the television set. It was absurd to be sitting there staring at the blank gray screen.

Nothing seemed real any more. He had, in a sense, been torn up by the roots.

He felt restless sitting down, so he got up and went into his bedroom—their bedroom, which was now his alone.

"Annette," he whispered.

And, as his daughter had done, he flung himself down full-length on the bed.

A little while later, Nathalie came to call him. In a daze, he went into the dining room, where the children were waiting for him. Alarmed at his appearance, they looked at him with ill-concealed anxiety.

"Let's start," he said, more loudly than necessary.

Afterward, he could not remember what he had eaten, except that there had been some small, highly spiced sausages.

"I don't suppose you want to watch television?" asked Marlène, rather subdued.

"Certainly not!"

Why not? He had no idea. He just didn't want to listen to music, still less to chattering voices.

"I'll say good night now, my dears. I'm going to bed."

"So early?"

"What else is there to do?"

Nathalie, as usual, had eaten with them at the table. She always managed to cook and serve the meal, and sit and share it with them.

"Good night, Nathalie."

"Would you like me to get you a hot drink?"

20

"Thanks, no."

"Why not take one of madame's tablets?"

Annette had suffered from fairly frequent bouts of insomnia, and their family physician, Doctor Bouchard, who was also a family friend, had prescribed a mild sedative.

The bottle stood on the little table in the bathroom. Célerin took two of the tablets; then, catching a glimpse of himself in the mirror, he gave a start at the sight of his ravaged face. It was as though some vital spark had been extinguished in him, leaving only a pale, restless ghost of a man.

He undressed, brushed his teeth, and got into the double bed, which now seemed much too spacious.

"No, Georges . . . not tonight . . . I'm so tired."

She had said that so often. But why, now that the business was doing so well, did she still cling so obstinately to her job as a social worker? It would not have been so bad if she had worked in an office. But no. Every day she went on her rounds, visiting the aged, the sick, and the helpless. Not only did she sit and chat with them to raise their spirits; she also washed them, did their housework, and, in many cases, cooked their meals.

Most of her "clients," as she affectionately called them, lived on the fifth or sixth floor of a tenement, and there were, of course, no elevators.

He had said, when they became engaged:

"I hope you aren't thinking of keeping your job after we're married?"

"Listen to me, Georges, don't you ever say that again. If you were to force me to choose between you and my work, I don't know what I'd do. . . ."

She was slightly built, not tall, but with an inexhaustible fund of energy. Her father had died in a German

21

concentration camp, and her mother was living out what was left of her life in an old people's home in the suburbs. Annette seldom went to see her. He had sensed that she felt a sort of resentment toward her mother, but he had not ventured to probe further.

The fact was that they talked very little. They lived together in affectionate harmony. What more could they want? Occasionally, Annette would come out with some story about one of her clients, but not often.

Most, if not all, of them must have experienced moments of happiness. Now they were just derelicts, awaiting death in their separate garrets.

And yet how tenaciously they clung to life!

"If you could see the way they look at me when I come in . . . I'm all they have left."

"I understand."

He understood, and at the same time he did not—not entirely, at any rate.

"You're ruining your health . . ."

"I've never felt better."

It was true. She had never been ill. There was nothing wrong with her, except for the occasional sleepless night.

And now she was dead because she had darted out into the road at a run. It was typical of her. She was always in a rush. She had spent the whole of her life running around. Had she had any idea what all the rush was about?

He thought he heard the telephone ring, but the sound was far off, muffled, and he made no move to get out of bed.

He must have slept, perhaps even dreamed, because the next thing he knew, Nathalie's bulky form was bending over him, as she always bent over the children at least once during the night.

22

He was thankful not to have awakened in an empty room. Nathalie put his cup of coffee down on the bedside table, and touched him on the shoulder.

"Monsieur."

He groaned.

"It's nine o'clock."

"Yes."

It meant nothing to him.

"Your partner is waiting for you in the living room."

"Who?"

"Monsieur Brassier."

Nathalie did not like him; he had no idea why. Brassier and his wife came to dinner from time to time, and on these occasions Nathalie was always grouchy, which was quite out of character.

"Have some coffee."

He sat up with difficulty, and put out a rather shaky hand for the cup.

"You had been drinking before you got home yesterday, hadn't you?"

No one else would have dared to question him in this way. Not even Annette herself.

He felt himself blushing, and muttered:

"Yes . . . I was at the end of my rope . . . I went into the bistro up the road . . . Chez Léon."

"How many drinks did you have?"

"Three."

"I want you to promise me that you won't do it again. You're not used to liquor. In your present state, after the shock you've had, it could do you a lot of harm . . ."

"I didn't know what I was doing . . . I just had this urge, all of a sudden."

"I'll get your breakfast while you have a shower and dress. Monsieur Brassier can wait."

He did as he was told, as though she were his mother or his nurse.

In the living room, he found his partner reading the morning paper. He jumped to his feet and gripped Célerin by the shoulders.

"I'm so terribly sorry, my dear boy. I don't know what to say, but you can imagine how I feel. I thought the world of Annette, you know that, and when they told me yesterday at the shop . . ."

Nathalie cut him short with the announcement that breakfast was ready.

"Thanks . . . You'll have a cup of coffee with me, won't you?"

"I've just had breakfast. I only dropped in to see how you were. Where are the children?"

"At school, I suppose."

"Did they feel up to it?"

"I don't know. I just took it for granted. . . . I shall be going to work myself, shortly."

At this, Brassier seemed a little taken aback.

"When will they be bringing her home?"

"I don't know . . . I don't know anything. I only saw her for a moment in the hospital corridor."

"What arrangements are you making?"

"I really don't know . . . I don't know how these things are done."

A shaft of sunlight struck across the tablecloth as he chewed his croissants, unconscious of what he was eating.

"You can do one of two things. You can have her brought back here, and then people can call to pay their last respects . . ."

"Yes, I suppose that would be best . . ."

"Or you can arrange for the undertakers to keep her in a memorial chapel until the funeral."

"What do you think?"

24

"It's up to you. It rather depends on when she can be removed from the Forensic Laboratory, and on the date of the funeral."

"What do you mean?"

"I'm thinking of the children. If it's a question of having to keep her here in the apartment for two or three days, it would be an ordeal for them."

"Yes, I see . . ."

"Was she a Catholic?"

"No. She was never even baptized. Her father was a teacher, and a fanatical freethinker, as they used to be called."

"And you?"

"I'm not what you would call a practicing Christian."

"Then you won't want a church service . . . unless you think it might cause talk among the neighbors?"

Célerin had no views either way. He watched Brassier pacing up and down as he talked. In the face of his intense vitality, Célerin felt ashamed of his own apathy.

"Can I help in any way? Would you like me to go and see the undertakers for you? Do you have a family vault?"

"A family vault for the Célerins! You're joking. My parents were peasants, and they were buried in the graveyard behind the village church."

"Haven't you even bought a plot?"

"No."

"Did Annette take out any life insurance?"

"No. I'm the one who's insured, with Annette and the children as the beneficiaries. I took out the policy when we were first married, and I increased it when . . ."

"What about claims against the truck driver?"

"They say it was not his fault. It was she who slipped and practically threw herself under the wheels."

"That's no reason why . . . There'll be an inquest . . ."

Brassier was a born organizer It was the same in business. He was the one who attended to all the practical details, the correspondence, and so on.

"If they start asking questions, just say you don't know a thing."

He shrugged, and finished his third cup of coffee.

"I don't know which cemetery it will be . . . all the cemeteries in and around Paris are filled to capacity."

Once again he shrugged. What did it matter where her body was buried, since Annette herself was no longer there?

The telephone rang. He picked up the receiver.

"Yes . . . Who? Yes . . . I am Georges Célerin . . . her husband. Yes. As soon as convenient?"

Still holding the receiver to his ear, he turned to Brassier.

"Yes . . . I'll make the necessary arrangements, but I'll have to make some inquiries first. Will this afternoon be soon enough? . . . Thank you."

He hung up. He felt he was being pushed, and he hated it It was as though he were losing Annette all over again.

"Who was it?"

"The Forensic Laboratory . . . She can be taken away as soon as arrangements can be made."

"What have you decided?"

"I'm not sure."

"Shall I go, to give you time to think it over?"

"No. It had better be the undertakers."

He was thinking of the children, and of himself, too, perhaps. She was dead. What were the alternatives? To lay her out on their bed, or put her on view to the public in the living room?

"Let's go."

2

Perhaps it had been a mistake to leave it all to the undertakers. A bare cubicle with no crucifix, no sprig of rosemary dipped in holy water. He could feel Nathalie's disapproval. Even the children had been put out. And the other tenants, the neighbors, could not understand why there had been no church service.

It had hardly seemed like a real funeral.

Had he changed in some way? It was hard to tell. Jean-Jacques and Marlène no longer looked at him in quite the old way. It was as though they could not make him out.

He was no longer just an ordinary man and a father. He had become a widower, and he felt ill at ease in his new role.

Before the funeral in the cemetery at Ivry, Brassier had attended to all the formalities. It was he who, after having read through it very carefully, had advised him to sign the form renouncing all legal claims against the owners of the van.

He knew he was being watched. It surprised them, he supposed, to see him looking so exhausted. His assistants could see it in the way he did his work. All his enthusiasm and self-confidence seemed to have evaporated. It was no good, they realized, talking to him, trying to take him out of himself.

27

"What about sending out for a bottle, *patron?*"

"If you like."

But he did not drink any of the Beaujolais that Pierrot went out to buy.

What they did not seem to realize, what nobody, not even Nathalie or his own children realized, was that he would never be the same man again. How had it been possible, he wondered, for him to live for so many years in a state of almost childlike euphoria?

It was a dull, monochrome existence, centered from morning to night upon someone who was no longer there.

And yet, oddly enough, in spite of this he felt that his wife was closer to him than she had been when she was alive.

Certainly, he had been a good husband, or at least so he had believed. He had done all he could. He had never been seriously interested in any other woman. He had loved Annette with all his heart.

He had never denied her anything she wanted, and whenever a difference of opinion had arisen, he had always given in to her.

Now, it was as if she had been absorbed into his being, and every minute of their life together had become a part of him.

From time to time, suddenly, he would recall some incident from the past; to his associates, who were covertly watching him, he seemed at such moments like a sleepwalker awakening.

Their first holiday together, for instance, which had also been their honeymoon. Except to go to Nevers or Caen, where their parents lived, neither of them had ever traveled before.

They had decided to spend three days in Nice; not a particularly original choice, but they had always wanted to see the Mediterranean.

On the train, he had awakened at the crack of dawn in a state of high excitement. He had seen the sun rise over a fairy-tale landscape dominated by almond trees in full bloom.

He had never seen an almond tree, except on a calendar. Annette, when he had woken her, had not been quite so thrilled, but she had joined him at the window, and pressed her forehead to the glass.

They had seen their first cacti, then their first palm trees. He had taken her hand. She had surrendered it to him absent-mindedly. This he realized for the first time, for all these vivid recollections had been dormant in his memory until now.

They had gone to the restaurant car for breakfast. Neither had ever before had a meal served on a train.

"Are you happy?"

"Yes."

Suddenly there was the blue sea, as blue as on a postcard, with little white fishing boats dotted about.

He was beginning to discover, now that she was dead, that in all their twenty years together he had never really known her. That was what he was doing now, reluctantly. He was, in a sense, trying to get to know her in retrospect.

The hotel in Nice had a sea front. He had watched her while she unpacked their things. He never tired of looking at her.

"Come and look."

"In a minute."

There had been a large steamer on the horizon. She had crossed over to the window and stood beside him for a minute or two. No doubt she had not wished to appear ungracious. And that night he had suffered a slight disappointment. A great disappointment, if the truth were told, which had insidiously undermined the whole of their married life.

He had made love to her with great tenderness, but had been unable to awaken in her the smallest tremor of pleasure. Her face had been very close to his, and it had been wholly without expression.

In spite of himself, he had felt a pang of distress because she could not share his pleasure.

But was it so very unusual? Much the same thing had happened to friends of his, but it had all come right in the end.

"Shall we go for a walk along the Promenade des Anglais?"

She had agreed, without enthusiasm. She had not even taken his arm as they walked side by side.

"It's beautiful."

He had dreaded the coming night, wondering whether he was perhaps to blame. Maybe, in the intensity of his own feelings, he had been clumsy?

She still did not respond, but afterward she had smiled at him as though he were a child.

"Have I disappointed you?"

"No."

"I can't help myself, Georges. Perhaps I'm not like other women. I hope I may improve as time goes on."

"But of course. The great thing is not to let it worry you."

He was forever thinking of little ways of pleasing her, and her response was always to reward him with an absent smile.

Their relationship had been almost platonic. Except in the bedroom, she was her old familiar self, and after a few months, she even seemed to respond a little to his love-making.

Even so, she had always locked the bathroom door. He had never seen her in the bath or under the shower. In fact, he had never seen her naked for more than a second or two.

She had returned to work, and her energy was remarkable, in contrast to her frail appearance.

"There's no need for you to work. I'm earning enough to keep us both."

He was still working on Rue Saint-Honoré, and was making very good money. They were living in the apartment on Boulevard Beaumarchais, and were planning to expand into the apartment next door. They had no children yet.

Would they ever have any? At that time, Georges was beginning to doubt it. The prospect of a childless marriage disturbed him.

"Do you like children, Annette?"

"Of course. Who doesn't?"

"That's not what I mean. I mean would you like children of your own, our children?"

"Why shouldn't I?"

He had not been unhappy. He had never been unhappy until that moment, such a very short time ago, when he had caught sight of a policeman's cap through the half-open workshop door.

He had had her. Surely that was all that mattered? And furthermore, after three years, she had announced that she was pregnant. And on that occasion, she really had been radiating happiness.

"I do hope it will be a boy."

"Whichever it is, it will still be ours. And we can have others."

"I'd like the eldest to be a boy. I don't want a lot of children, two maybe, a boy and a girl."

During the whole of her pregnancy, he had not touched her, partly from a kind of reverence for her condition, and partly because he felt he should not interfere in any way with the processes of gestation.

"I do hope that after this you won't go back to work."

"Not for the first few weeks perhaps, but I couldn't stand just sitting around doing nothing forever."

She would not take advice. Her mind was made up.

It was just before this time that they had engaged Nathalie, who had immediately taken over the running of the household. Annette had no interest whatsoever in housekeeping. She did not even bother to discuss the menus with Nathalie. She had kept on with her work right up to the last month. It was almost as though she were defying him.

Still, he had been happy, and at the time it had all seemed quite natural. It was only now, looking back, that he was beginning to wonder, in an effort to understand Annette as she really was.

It had been a boy. He would have liked him to be called Georges, after himself; or if not, Patrick, a name of which he was particularly fond.

"No. We'll call him Jean-Jacques."

He had raised no objection. By this time he had set up on his own on Rue de Sévigné in partnership with Jean-Paul Brassier. As a young man, he had dreamed of becoming a sculptor. He had come to Paris, intending to enroll at the École des beaux-arts, no matter what he might be forced to do to keep himself, even if it meant working in Les Halles, unloading crates of fruit and vegetables all through the night.

It was a notice in the Help Wanted column of a newspaper that had altered the whole course of his life. There was a vacancy for an apprentice goldsmith at a jeweler's on Rue Saint-Honoré. Although he had thought that he was probably too young, he had applied for the job.

After only a few weeks, he was being entrusted with work requiring a high degree of skill, and after three years, when the head of the workshop retired, he was promoted to his job.

At a small party given by a married friend in his apartment on Avenue d'Orléans he had met Annette. It was the first time he had ever been to a private party. Like everyone else, he had a few drinks, and it seemed to him that his glass was never empty.

There had been dancing to the music of a record player. At some stage, he had gone up to a girl who had been sitting alone, watching the others gyrating.

"Would you care to dance?"

"No."

Although her manner had been far from encouraging, he had sat down beside her.

"Have you known our host long?"

"This is the first time I've been here. The only people I know are our host and Lypsky, that little man with red hair. He brought me here. He and I have rooms in the same house."

"Have you always lived in Paris?"

"No. I was born in a village near Nevers."

"Have you been long in Paris?"

"You're very inquisitive!"

Emboldened by wine, he had answered:

"I'm just making conversation."

"That's honest, at any rate. It doesn't really matter to you whether I was born in Nevers or Biarritz."

"As it happens, you could be a Basque, with your black hair and brown eyes. Why aren't you dancing?"

"I don't care for it. It seems to me rather ridiculous, people looking into each other's faces, and jiggling up and down . . ."

"Do you have a job?"

"Yes."

33

"In an office?"

"No."

"In a shop?"

"No. You needn't go on. You'd never guess. I'm a social worker."

"What does that mean, exactly?"

"We visit old people, those who are housebound or handicapped in other ways. We concentrate on the poorest section of the community, especially those who have no one else to turn to. We wash them and cook for them, and do a bit of housework . . ."

"It must be very hard work."

"No. Not when you're used to it."

"Isn't it demoralizing to see so many people living in conditions like that?"

"They themselves are not demoralized. They're a cheerful lot, on the whole, apart from the occasional suicide. And it's mostly the younger ones who commit suicide . . . the older ones know better."

He could remember every single word of their conversation.

As they were all leaving, he had said:

"May I hope to see you again?"

"Why do you ask?"

"I'm one of the lonely ones myself."

She had not asked him anything about himself.

"My address is Hotel du Grand-Ours, Rue Saint-Jacques."

Afterward, it had all seemed like a dream recollected through a haze of wine. He was sure he would never see her again, and he did not greatly care.

She was different from other girls. She had chosen a very demanding career, more demanding than any other, perhaps, and yet she had spoken of it with enthusiasm.

Two or three weeks had gone by. He had forgotten to ask her name but, fortunately, the friend who had given the party was able to help him.

"Her name is Annette Delaine. But if you're seriously interested, I should warn you that you won't get anywhere with her . . . you won't be the first to have tried . . .

"How well do you know her?"

"We come from the same village; her father was teacher there. We were at school together. She's younger than I am, and I used to treat her like a kid sister. Not any more, though . . . I wouldn't dare."

One evening, he had bought some theater tickets and knocked on the door of her room on Rue Saint-Antoine.

"Who is it?"

"Georges Célerin."

"I don't know you."

"We met at Raoul's. We had quite a long chat."

"Why didn't you telephone first? There's a telephone in the house, didn't you know? What do you want?"

"I've got two tickets for the Comédie Française."

He had deliberately chosen a classical production. She looked at him curiously.

"You mean you bought them especially?"

He had blushed, tempted to pretend that they had been given to him, but in the end had mumbled:

"Yes."

"Not knowing whether or not I would agree to come, or even if I was at home?"

"Yes."

"What's on?"

"A Feydeau farce, and *Le Malade Imaginaire*."

"Wait for me downstairs. I'll be ready in a quarter of an hour."

That had been the real beginning. She had tolerated

35

him. Occasionally, she had allowed him to take her to the theater, or even to the movies if there was a really interesting film showing. Afterward, they would go to a snack bar for a glass of beer and a sandwich.

At the door of her lodgings, she would shake hands with him, friendly but uninvolved, and thank him for a pleasant evening.

Things had gone on in this way for over a year. Outwardly, their relationship was unchanged, but now she was never out of his thoughts. One winter evening, when the sidewalks were slippery with ice, she had absently taken his arm, and he had felt the warmth of her body close to his.

Falteringly, he had said:

"There's something I want to ask you, but I know the answer will be no."

"What is it?"

"Would you consider marrying me? I'm not rich by any means, but I earn a good living, and I'm thinking of setting up on my own in the near future."

"Would you be very unhappy if I said no?"

"Yes."

"And if we were married, you wouldn't object to my going on working?"

What could he say, however unwillingly, but that he would not?

"Well then, my answer is I'll think about it."

"When can I see you again?"

"Soon. But you must give me time to think."

She had said, "I'll think about it." He was on top of the world. That night, his hotel room seemed to him a palace.

It was true that he was already thinking of setting up on his own. Brassier had not yet come forward with his offer. He planned to rent a workshop in the goldsmiths' quarter, in the general neighborhood of Rue des Francs-Bourgeois. He would do everything himself. As he saw it, the goldsmith's craft was very much akin to that of the sculptor of his boyhood dreams.

He would make jewelry from his own original designs, quite different from the kind of thing he had had to produce as an employee. And, little by little, he would build up a clientele.

He had found a woman who was willing to entrust herself to him, who would give him companionship and understanding. He could scarcely believe his luck.

He had waited three weeks before telephoning.

"Have you had your dinner?"

"Not yet."

"How would you like to have dinner with me? So far, you haven't."

"How soon will you be here?"

"In half an hour. Will that be all right?"

"Yes."

He had taken her to a restaurant on Place des Vosges, which he had often seen from the outside. He had never had a meal there; it had looked too expensive.

They had sat facing one another at a small table for two. Annette had put on rather more make-up than usual, and she was wearing a blue dress with a white collar. He remembered it very well.

"The *andouillettes* are underlined in red on the menu. They must be a specialty of the house."

"I adore *andouillettes*."

He could remember everything, every word they had said to one another. He could even remember the couple at the next table. The man had been fat, with a thick neck and a blotchy complexion. The woman was almost as fat, and wore a diamond of at least nine carats.

"Don't you want to know what I've decided?"

They had drunk *vin rosé*, only a little, but enough to make them feel warm inside.

"I don't dare ask. It's been such a marvelous evening, I don't want to spoil it."

"What if I said yes?"

"You don't mean . . . ?"

He almost leaped out of his seat and kissed her on both cheeks.

"Yes, I do. You're a good man and I'm very fond of you. We'll always be the best of friends."

At the time, he had not paid much attention to her words. Now they came back to him, and set him wondering.

"Are you glad?"

"I'm the happiest of men."

"We'll have to find somewhere to live first."

"I'll start looking tomorrow . . . What part of town would you prefer?"

"This district . . . it's where I work . . . I've got used to it."

She was dead, and in twenty years of marriage he had understood nothing.

"We'll always be the best of friends."

Was that not exactly what they had been?

"Would you mind if I ordered a bottle of champagne?"

"Not so long as I can take my time drinking it."

He had called the wine waiter. A few minutes later, a silver bucket was brought to the table, with the neck of the bottle sticking out. He had never before ordered champagne in a restaurant, though he had had it once or twice.

"To our life together, Annette."

"Cheers."

They had clinked glasses and drunk, looking into one another's eyes.

Afterward he had taken her back to her room.

"Tonight you may kiss me."

He had kissed her on the cheeks, and barely touched her lips with his.

"When shall I see you again?"

"Next Wednesday?"

"Shall we go out to dinner again?"

"Yes, but somewhere less expensive."

And after a pause, she had added:

"And no more champagne."

These evocations of the past did not prevent him from noticing, almost in spite of himself, all that was going on around him. He himself would have preferred life to come to a stop. He wished that Annette's death had brought about the end of the world; yet when he returned to his workshop on Rue de Sévigné, he looked out through the skylight and saw pink chimney pots and gray rooftops silhouetted against a powder blue sky in which no cloud had appeared for several days past.

He had a friendly word for everyone, and no doubt gave the impression that he was feeling better.

He went to his drawing board and completed the sketch of the brooch he had been working on when the police sergeant had arrived to break the tragic news to him. Every line was drawn with love, as though it were a memorial to Annette.

She was not dead to him, and sometimes, in the apartment on Boulevard Beaumarchais, he would turn with some remark on his lips, only to recall that she was no longer there.

With the children and also with Nathalie he was now

less withdrawn, but this was merely because old habits were beginning to reassert themselves.

One evening, when he was alone with his son, Jean-Jacques asked, as though it were the most natural thing in the world:

"Tell me, Father, have you ever thought of marrying again?"

It was plain that he would have no objection, that, on the contrary, he would probably be content to see another woman in his mother's place.

"No, son, I never have."

"Why not?"

"I loved your mother too much."

"That's no reason to be miserable all by yourself for the rest of your life. There will come a time, not so very far ahead, when I shall leave home. And, later, Marlène will get married. That will leave no one but Nathalie to take care of you, and she's getting on, she won't be able to work forever . . ."

"You're very thoughtful, and I'm grateful, but no one could take your mother's place."

He was taken aback by this conversation. Whoever would have thought that a sixteen-year-old boy would have been so very down to earth? It was his mother who had died, and yet he could talk about his father's remarriage as though it were the most natural thing in the world.

The trees were coming into leaf. The streets seemed livelier, now that the men were leaving their overcoats at home and the women going out in gaily colored dresses.

He remembered how he had found the apartment. By then, he had grown very friendly with Jean-Paul Brassier, the salesman at the firm he worked for. He was addressed respectfully by everyone as Monsieur Brassier, no doubt as a tribute to his quite remarkable self-assurance.

He was a young man for whom life would always be easy. He was the first to be told of Cèlerin's forthcoming marriage.

"What! You too!" exclaimed Brassier.

"You've met her. She was at that housewarming party of Raoul's a year ago. Speaking of housewarming, I'll have to start looking for an apartment. We can't get married until we have somewhere to live."

"The best thing is to go to a real-estate agent."

A fortnight later, he was offered the apartment on Boulevard Beaumarchais. He was delighted with it. Admittedly, it had only two rooms, besides the bathroom and a tiny kitchen, but they were quite a decent size.

"I've got a surprise for you. What do you think it is?"

She had smiled.

"I can guess."

"What is it, then?"

"An apartment in this district. Near where I work, and not too far for you."

He was bubbling over with happiness, because he could no longer bear to be parted from her, even for a day. Her presence was absolutely necessary to him. Had it been possible, he would never have left her, from morning to night and from night to morning.

"Whereabouts is it?"

"On Boulevard Beaumarchais. It's a bit on the small side, but it's only temporary, anyway . . ."

It was eight o'clock in the evening, too late to expect the concierge to show them around. They had dinner in a little restaurant they had discovered on Rue de Béarn. It was old-fashioned, with a genuine zinc bar and frilly paper tablecloths. The kitchen door was always left open, and one could see the proprietor's wife preparing the food.

"Would you like to have a look at it tomorrow?"

"It will have to be early. I've got a very busy day."

He, too, had a busy day ahead, but surely the apartment—in other words their marriage—ought to come first?

"What time would suit you?"

"Eight o'clock."

"I'll come and get you. I'll be waiting for you downstairs."

Now, looking back after twenty years, he was sure that she had not shared his excitement. He could not understand it. The concierge, who had short legs, was called Madame Molard.

"So you're the young lady this gentleman is going to marry? Well, he's not doing too badly for himself. You're a pretty girl, all right."

She went up with them to the third floor, opened the door, and left them.

"Of course a room never looks much without furniture. But we'll buy furniture. I've got quite a bit of money saved . . ."

"It's fine," she had said, leaning on the window sill and looking out at a dense screen of branches and leaves.

"Aren't you going to kiss me?"

"Of course."

"This should be the bedroom. The other room is bigger . . . we'll have to eat in there as well. At first we'll get just the basic furniture, and then gradually we can replace it with something better."

"After all the slum living I've seen, I'm not fussy."

"Not fussy"—the phrase had not made any particular impression on him at the time; but now, recalling it, it seemed charged with significance.

"It shouldn't take more than a couple of weeks to get everything we need."

"What's the hurry?"

"It can't be too soon. I think of nothing else all day."

During those two weeks, he had, in fact, been absent a good deal from the workshop on Rue Saint-Honoré. Fortunately for him, his employer had been sympathetic, and left him to his own devices.

He had gone to one of the large stores and found most of what he needed in the furniture department.

"What about household linen?"

He had gone down to the linen department, and bought sheets, pillowcases, towels, and bath mats. It had cost him the greater part of his savings.

But now he could get married! Everything was ready.

"I'll come and meet you tomorrow morning. I've got a surprise for you."

On the landing he had told her to close her eyes. Leading her by the hand, he had taken her into the living room, which was now fully furnished, even down to a television set.

"Now you can open them."

"You didn't waste any time . . ."

"Well, you see, all this is just makeshift. Do you like old furniture, the kind one still sometimes sees in the home of a provincial lawyer, for instance?"

"I do."

"That's what we'll have eventually. I want nothing but the best for you."

She had looked up at him with a slight smile, in

43

which there was no doubt some affection, but also perhaps a hint of irony. Who could tell?

"Is there anyone you'd like to have as bridesmaid and witness at the ceremony?"

"My boss is no longer a spring chicken, and she looks like a horse."

"Well, look. I have a friend, a man called Brassier. He's been married two years, and his wife is very attractive. I'll introduce you to them both. You can ask his wife to be your witness, and I'll ask him to be mine."

Eveline Brassier was more than just attractive. She was beautiful—tall and slender, with delicately modeled features framed in long, naturally blonde hair.

She moved gracefully, but was always a little languid; in other words, a hothouse rather than an open-air plant.

Célerin invited them to dine at the restaurant on Place des Vosges. Brassier had a red two-seater Alpha Romeo, of which he was very proud.

"Well, when is it to be?"

Annette motioned toward Célerin.

"Ask him. He's making all the arrangements."

"The third week in March? Let's say the twenty-first. It's an easy date to remember for anniversaries."

"How many guests?" inquired Brassier.

"Just the four of us."

"What about family?"

"Both our parents live in the country, a long way from Paris. We want a quiet wedding."

And it had been just that, sandwiched between two other weddings in the *mairie* of the Third Arrondissement. They had lunched on Place des Vosges, and, on this occasion, Annette had not protested when he ordered champagne with the dessert.

Cèlerin had been happy. He had been full of his own happiness. From now on he would be living with her. He would see her every day, at breakfast, lunch, and dinner, and he would be sleeping next to her at night.

That same evening, they had taken the Blue Train to Nice. His happiness had persisted. He was living in a dream, in spite of his wife's frigidity.

"It will come right in time."

Just as, in time, after their return to Paris, they had settled down into a routine. They could not afford a maid. That would have to wait. Annette was working practically the whole day. They used to meet for lunch at one or another of the many small restaurants in the neighborhood. In time, they got to know them all.

In the evening, his wife got home before he did, just in time to prepare a simple meal. In the summer, they usually had a cold supper.

"Don't you think we ought to go and see our families?"

They had taken a couple of days off from work. The village, in Nièvre, was gay and colorful. Annette's father, a tall, raw-boned man with a pointed beard, greeted them with a powerful handshake.

"Well, my boy, I'm delighted to have you for a son-in-law. I can't think how you managed it. Speaking for myself, I've never been able to get ten consecutive words out of her . . ."

A bottle of the local white wine appeared on the table. Annette's mother came from the kitchen with the food.

"I hope you'll spend the night with us? We've kept Annette's bedroom just as it was. It's never used."

It was a moving experience to sleep in the room that had been hers throughout her childhood and adolescence. The bed was on the small side for two, but they made do with it.

45

"May I?" he asked, pointing to the handle of a drawer.

"I doubt if there's anything in it."

There was. School notebooks filled with very small but remarkably neat handwriting.

"Did you do well at school?"

"I was always at the top of the class."

The room was papered in a design of multicolored flowers. Célerin had been much taken with the chest of drawers, but had not had the nerve to ask if they might take it to Paris with them.

They had left in the early afternoon by the small local train to Nevers, where they caught their connection to Paris.

The visit had not been a disappointment. Nothing had ever disappointed him in those days. He was flooded by happiness. Had it not continued that way all along? Not exuberance, exactly. He had talked very little. But he had savored every minute, like a child with an ice-cream cone.

At last he had attained perfect happiness, or so it felt to him.

"Are you happy?"

"Why do you keep asking? Not just once a day, but three, four times . . ."

"Because I want you to be as happy as I am."

"I am happy."

But she did not say it as he would have said it. In the evenings, she would rather watch television than talk. Sitting beside her, he had spent as much time looking at her as at the screen. Finally it irritated her.

"Have I a smudge on my face?"

"No."

"Then why do you keep turning around and looking at me?"

She did not seem to understand that he adored her. After a year, they still had no children. From time to time, they went to dinner with the Brassiers on Avenue de Versailles. The Brassiers kept a maid, and it had distressed him not to be able to do as much for his wife.

On Sundays the Brassiers went for long drives in the country. Often they would start out on Saturday afternoon, and spend the night at some quaint little inn.

When the Célerins entertained them, it always had to be in a restaurant. Annette could not cook, as she had frankly admitted to him before they were married.

"I can just about boil or fry an egg."

They spent their Sundays wandering about Paris, getting to know the back streets or walking slowly along the crowded Champs-Élysées.

If the weather was bad, they went to a movie.

Had it not been a somewhat bleak life for a young woman? But what else was there for them to do without a car? He had worked as much overtime as he could, determined to save for a car, not an Alpha Romeo—at any rate, not to begin with—but some cheap little secondhand model.

She had never uttered a word of complaint. She often smiled to herself, apparently at her own thoughts.

"What are you thinking about?"

"Nothing in particular. About you . . . all the little things you do to please me."

One scorching weekend in the middle of summer, they had gone to visit his father. They took the train to Caen, and had to wait a long time for the local train to his home village, which was really not much more than a hamlet.

The "farm" was an old thatched cottage with an adjoining field, where three cows were kept, and a sow, running free with her piglets.

His father was a stocky man of peasant build, with the telltale high color of the heavy drinker. His wife was dead, and he was looked after by an old woman servant.

"Well, well! If it isn't sonny boy!"

But he had such a thick accent that the words were scarcely intelligible. Although the house was clean, a faint whiff of cow dung drifted into the kitchen.

"And this, I take it, is the wife you wrote to me about?"

"This is my wife, yes."

"Not bad. A bit skinny for my taste, if you want the truth, but a nice little piece of fluff . . ."

With ritual solemnity, he had gone to the sideboard, taken out a bottle of Calvados, and filled four glasses.

"That's Justine over there," he mumbled, pointing at her. "When she lost her husband, she had nowhere to go, so I said she could come here."

Justine looked like a crow, and so far had not dared open her mouth.

"Well, here's to us all!"

He emptied his glass in a single gulp. Annette choked on the stuff, which was ninety proof. The old man distilled it himself.

"Too strong for her, is it? A tame little town mouse, isn't she?"

"As a matter of a fact, she's from the country, same as we are."

"Where from?"

"Near Nevers."

"I don't know nothing about such faraway places."

He looked the young woman up and down from top to toe, as he would have scrutinized a cow at a fair, and his glance came to rest on her middle.

"No bun in the oven yet?"

She flushed. He could sense her distress. His father refilled the glasses. He must have had at least a couple of drinks before they arrived.

It distressed him, too, that the visit should be a failure, but they had to stay on, waiting for the local train.

"It's milking time. Justine!"

In two hours, his father had had six glasses of Calvados, and when he got up, he was swaying so much that, for a moment, he had to hold on to the table.

"Don't worry about me. I'm still capable of putting away a whole bottle."

He went off into the field and never saw them leave, because by that time he was snoring in the long grass under the blazing sun.

"I'm so sorry."

"What about?"

"To have subjected you to such a spectacle. I felt we had to come just this once . . . the way he's going, I doubt if he'll last much longer."

"You know, Georges, he's not the first I've seen. Remember, I'm a country girl, too, and show me the village that hasn't got its drunk. And I've had to handle them in Paris, too, in the course of my work."

"How do you deal with them?"

"First I give them a good rubdown, then I make them some hot coffee, forcing it down, if necessary, and I leave something for them to eat on the table."

Was it that she felt she had a vocation? Her work seemed to mean more to her than her marriage. He had never dared to speak to her about it, feeling that the subject was somehow taboo.

She was an agnostic, so she could not have been motivated by religious faith. Was it that she loved people? Or that she was sorry for them? Or simply that she wanted to be of use? He had not known the answer then, and he still did not know it. Now that she was dead, he would never know.

He had shared his life with her for twenty years. They had had lunch together almost every day, and had spent all their evenings and nights together.

What did he know? The more the past came back to him, in disjointed fragments, the more it confused him. Yet, he needed to understand. He gave all his mind to it, setting one event against another, in the hope of striking some spark of illumination.

It was for this that she had to be kept alive, and it was he alone who could save her from extinction.

As long as he kept a place for her in his heart, some part of her, at least, would still live on.

As far as the children were concerned, she already belonged to the past, and they could talk about her objectively, almost as though she were a stranger. Had not Jean-Jacques calmly discussed the possibility of replacing her?

It was shortly after their visit to his father that Brassier had invited him to lunch, just the two of them on their own.

"What's he after?"

"I've no idea."

"I'd be careful, if I were you. He could so easily overreach you. Besides, he's immensely ambitious. Nothing counts for him but success at all costs."

3

Brassier had taken him to one of the smartest restaurants in Paris, which had made Célerin feel uncomfortable. It was typical of the man. He had this childish need to impress, which caused him to have his suits made by a first-class tailor, and to buy his ties on Place Vendôme.

They were presented with a cart loaded with hors d'oeuvres, more than twenty different kinds. Célerin was at a loss what to choose. There were things that he had never seen before, such as little dark green bundles, which turned out to be stuffed vine leaves.

Had his predicament been a source of amusement to Brassier? Very possibly. It would have been in character.

During the hors d'oeuvres, he talked idly of this and that. By the time the lamb chops arrived, Célerin no longer had any appetite.

"I wanted this chance to have a talk with you, just the two of us, because I've got big plans."

"Plans for whom?"

"For you and me. You're the finest craftsman in the firm, if not in the whole of Paris."

He shook his head deprecatingly.

"But it's true, you are! I sell twice as many of your things as anybody else's—and that in spite of the fact that you aren't really given a free hand. You have a style all your own, and the customers go for it."

He pushed his plate away, and lit a cigarette with a gold lighter.

"As to myself, I know I'm a born salesman, none better."

It was true. He was not exaggerating.

"I've just been left a tidy little sum of money. An aunt of mine—I was her only living relative—hoarded her money all her life. She denied herself everything, because, as she put it, 'I'm saving for my old age.' At the age of eighty-eight, she was still saving . . ."

Brassier smiled as he puffed at his cigarette.

"What I have in mind is that we should go into partnership."

"I've no money."

"We can manage without it. I have enough. You'll be virtually self-employed, like most other goldsmiths and diamond setters. I already have some premises in view. We should start small, I think, with just one or two assistants and an apprentice."

For Célerin it had been almost a historic occasion. Suddenly the opulence of the restaurant no longer troubled him, but that might have been because they had just finished one bottle of wine, and another was being uncorked.

"The workshop will be your responsibility, and I'll see to it that we get the customers. I'll pay you a salary, the same as you're getting at Schwartz's, but, on top of that, you'll be entitled to twenty-five per cent of the profits."

Célerin was at a loss for words. It was too good to be true. He had always dreamed of having his own little workshop, even if it meant doing everything himself.

52

"I don't expect an answer right away. Think it over for a day or two. All the same, I'd like you to have a look at the premises I have in mind."

Célerin got into the Alfa Romeo. Brassier had let down the roof, and they drove in the open car toward Rue des Francs-Bourgeois. They climbed the four flights of stairs of the building on Rue de Sévigné, and Célerin felt like a child who had been shown a luscious cake.

"Later, we'll turn this into a showroom, with display cases for some of the best pieces, and we'll put a saleswoman in charge."

But what interested Célerin was the large room with the sloping studio skylight. He could already see himself working at his bench, with two or three fellow craftsmen.

"Let me know by Wednesday, or, if you'd rather, Thursday. I don't want to rush you."

He would have liked to say that he had already given it plenty of thought, and that he was prepared to take it on, but he wanted to discuss it with Annette first.

"The firm will be known as Brassier and Célerin."

"That's not right, as I shall only be . . ."

"I know what I'm doing."

He could not remember what they had had for dessert. He waited impatiently for Annette to get home. He was longing to tell her of the great upheaval that was about to take place in their humdrum life.

"Do you know what? I'm going to be my own boss . . ."

She looked at him, puzzled.

"How do you mean?"

"Brassier and I are going into partnership."

"Where will you get the money?"

"He's just been left some. My contribution will be my work. In addition to my salary, I shall get twenty-five per cent of the profits."

"If it makes you happy, I'm glad."

"We'll probably be able to afford a maid."

"Where would we put her?"

"I don't know, but that will sort itself out."

A month later, the showroom was ready, and the workshop fitted out with brand-new equipment.

Célerin had engaged Jules Daven, whom he knew by reputation.

And through Daven, he had found Raymond Létang.

He had given his notice to Monsieur Schwartz, who had wished him luck, not without a touch of irony.

The speed of events suddenly quickened. All the good things seemed to come at once. It was almost overwhelming. Their next-door neighbors left Boulevard Beaumarchais to go and live in the country. Célerin was able to take over their lease, and get permission to knock the walls down and combine two apartments into one.

"Do you see what this means, Annette?"

"Yes; we shall have more room."

The enlarged apartment seemed too big for just the two of them.

"When we have children, we'll have plenty of room for them."

Almost at once, Brassier had brought in a flood of orders. Célerin and his two assistants hardly had a breathing spell.

They kept the finest pieces to display in the showcases in the shop. By the end of the year, they were looking for a saleswoman to attend to customers and keep the books. It was Brassier, once again, who found Madame Coutance. They all took to her at once.

54

Had it not all been too good to be true? Célerin went about in a dream. At least he saw his way to making jewelry in a style that was really new—sculptured pieces, in which stones were used merely to enliven the worked gold.

Later, Pierrot joined them, and they all worked together happily as a team.

Brassier was seldom there. He dropped in two or three times a week, picking up samples to show to the various jewelers. He was always full of projects, as befitted a man of his importance.

"I'm having a house built near Rambouillet. I've had just about enough of Paris, and so has my wife."

"Whereabouts exactly?"

"A tiny little place, Saint-Jean-de-Morteau, right on the forest. When it's ready, we'll have a housewarming. You must both come . . ."

Célerin felt no twinge of envy He considered that he had the best of the bargain. For him, every new piece of jewelry he made was a step forward.

His old dreams of becoming a sculptor were beginning to be realized, albeit in another medium.

He advertised for a housekeeper in two of the daily newspapers, including the words: "To live as family."

And then another miracle occurred. The first applicant was none other than Nathalie.

"How many in the household?"

"Just the two of us . . . for the moment."

"I'm fond of children," she had said, with a pleasant foreign lilt to her voice.

For, in spite of having been educated in France, she had retained a slight Russian accent. It took her barely three days to get the household organized. First, she set about transforming the kitchen.

"You can't go on lunching every day in restaurants,

and dining out so often. At this rate, you'll soon find you've ruined your digestions."

She was very outspoken and, on occasion, could be quite authoritarian.

Annette did not mind in the least. It was as though nothing mattered to her but her work. All the rest she left to Nathalie.

Now, looking back, it was hard to believe that things had ever been otherwise.

When his wife became pregnant, his joy knew no bounds. She had had the baby in a clinic. He had been to see her twice a day, and stayed with her until he was turned out.

"You really must go now, Georges. The nurses all tease me about you."

"Why shouldn't I stay as long as they let me?"

It was a private clinic, and the visiting hours were not strictly enforced. He always arrived loaded with flowers and sweets for the nurses as well as for Annette.

Could anyone possibly have been happier?

Every time he saw him, Brassier inquired after Annette and the baby.

"You'll see him soon. Anyway, there's no reason why you shouldn't go and have a look at him in the clinic."

They had had him baptized at the Church of Saint-Denis-du-Saint-Sacrement, with Brassier as godfather and Jules Daven's wife as godmother.

Nathalie had been most anxious that they should all have lunch afterward at the apartment, and she did things admirably, as though she had been a cook all her life. Eveline Brassier had appeared in an extremely elegant creation, which would have attracted attention even at a grand society wedding.

She had very little to say for herself. She seemed to

live in a world of her own. Their house, near Rambouillet, was almost ready for occupancy.

Business was booming. Every day brought new customers.

"Mind you, I'm only taking orders for exclusive pieces now. That's the line we want to build up."

Their reputation was growing rapidly, and Madame Coutance was kept busy in the shop with customers, including Old Mother Papin, as they called her behind her back, who had become their best customer.

Madame Veuve Papin, née de Molincourt. The ball-bearings plant ran itself. All she had to do was rake in the profits.

She lived on Avenue Hoche, and spent most of her afternoons playing bridge.

It was all very pleasant and reassuring. Annette became pregnant again, but this time, she seemed less than delighted.

She gave birth to a daughter, Marlène, and they had exactly the same lunch as for Jean-Jacques' christening, and the same godfather and godmother.

From time to time, the Brassiers came to dinner at the flat, and Nathalie cooked Russian dishes for them.

In addition to his Alpha Romeo, Brassier had bought an eight-seater station wagon, in which, one Sunday, he drove the Célerins down to his country house.

It was built in farmhouse style, cozy without being too rustic. Furniture, pictures, and carpets were all in the very best of taste. The walls were painted white with an eggshell finish, with most of the furniture coverings to match.

They were taken on a tour of the house. The babies were not along. They had left them at home with Nathalie. She was so wrapped up in them that she resented it whenever Annette took them in her arms.

In due course, Célerin, too, had become the owner of a car, an ordinary mass-produced model. He used it mainly for attending auction sales outside Paris. He bought sparingly, not aspiring to rare and valuable items, but concentrating on old, well-made provincial pieces, which he polished up himself when he got them home.

Occasionally, Annette would attend a sale with him, but not often. Had she changed since she had become a mother twice over? Her expression had grown softer, and her eyes brighter. She seemed, at last, to be enjoying life, and not just her work in the slums, to which she still gave much of her time.

She always wore navy blue, having decided once and for all that no other color suited her, but her dresses were often relieved with white trimmings.

One day she had asked him point blank: "What do you think of Eveline?"

"I can't really say. She's not easy to get to know."

"If you had been unattached, would you ever have thought of marrying her?"

"No."

"But she is beautiful, you must admit."

"Not as beautiful as you are."

"That's nonsense. I'm no beauty. I may not be exactly plain, but no one would look at me twice. Eveline could have been a fashion model or a film star. For one thing, she's tall and slim, whereas I'm on the small side . . ."

"Why did you ask what I thought of her?"

"Because she was in my mind. . . She seldom comes into Paris, just twice a week to go to the hairdresser. She spends endless time beautifying herself, and yet she hardly ever sees a soul. She spends days on end playing records and reading magazines . . ."

"How do you know?"

58

"Jean-Paul told me."

"Isn't he happy in his marriage?"

"She probably is the right wife for him. An expensive ornament."

This had been years ago. He had not paid much attention at the time. Now the conversation came back to him in microscopic detail.

Annette had given him twenty years of happiness. Probably she herself had scarcely noticed it, wrapped up as she almost always was in her work.

Gradually, over the years, she had become more responsive to his love-making, but there had always been an awkwardness about her, a latent sense of guilt, perhaps. Sometimes when she was in his arms, he had seen tears in her eyes.

"Anything wrong?"

"Nothing . . . it's just that I'm happy."

There had been times when Célerin had been frightened by his own happiness. But was it, after all, so extraordinary? He was surrounded by happy people, Nathalie, Madame Coutance, his fellow craftsmen.

With each of them, he had a perfectly easy, unclouded relationship. As the cycle of the seasons unfolded, Célerin savored each in turn. Winter delighted him no less than summer.

Seen through the big studio skylight, the rooftops, the clouds, suffused with pink or heavy with rain, were familiar as old friends.

Then came the time when Jean-Jacques, raised on a cushion, sat at the dinner table with the grownups.

To be joined, a year or two later, by his sister.

"What's happened to my chicks?" Nathalie would ask quaintly when they were absent from the apartment.

They had made friends with the other children in the

block. Nathalie took them for walks in the Tuileries Garden.

Célerin took a holiday for the first time since going into partnership with Brassier. He rented a house in Riva-Bella, not far from Caen, and took the whole family, including, needless to say, Nathalie.

The children had played on the beach. Célerin and his wife had sat in deck chairs, gazing dreamily at the sea.

"A penny for your thoughts."

"I was thinking about my old people. They must be wondering what has become of me."

The Brassiers were in Cannes, and had hired a yacht.

Célerin had thought about Paris, his workshop and his fellow craftsmen. He was a poor swimmer. Nathalie did not swim at all, but kept an eye on them all from the shore.

By the evening, their clothes were always full of sand, and they had to take a shower before going to bed.

"One of these days, we'll have a place of our own."

"For three weeks in the summer? Who would look after it for the rest of the year? You would need a caretaker to keep the rooms aired . . ."

"Do you like it here?"

"The beach is perfect for the children. The water is none too warm, but it doesn't seem to worry them."

It had not been a total failure, but it could not exactly be termed a success. It was obvious that Annette was not enjoying it. She said very little. For the first time, she had the leisure to play with the children, but she left all that to Nathalie. Nor did she offer to do any cooking.

She must have been missing her work. It meant as much to her as Célerin's workshop meant to him.

There were days when he, too, found time heavy on his hands.

"There's a good film showing at the Casino."

"You know I hate going out in the evenings."

Perhaps, after all, she had not been bored. She had always preferred a quiet life, seeing very few people, apart from her "clients" in the slums.

Presumably, she had an intense inner life, but at this her husband could only guess.

"Sometimes before our next holiday, I suggest we take a look around Brittany, and see if we can find someplace we like better than Riva-Bella."

"Whatever you say."

It was not that she was apathetic, or even indifferent, but simply that, outside her professional life, she preferred to leave the decisions to others. She was the same about food.

"What will you have, Madame?"

"I really don't care. My husband will choose. He's the one who enjoys his food."

It was with a sigh of relief that they had returned to Paris. They were back in the old, familiar setting. Nathalie could not wait to plug in the vacuum cleaner and get rid of the dust that had accumulated in their absence.

They dined out in one of the little restaurants where they used to go before they were married.

He still remembered with emotion the day when she had said yes. He had stared at her in astonishment, unable to understand how such a woman could be willing to share her life with a man like him.

She had smiled, he remembered, and that had made him feel even more awkward.

Was it that she was more mature than he? Possibly. In her presence, he always seemed to act like a child.

Indeed, he felt like a child anyway. That was how he saw himself, and it was always something of a shock when people treated him as an adult.

Even his chosen craft was a kind of game. He roughed out his sketches as a child draws a house. And to make a piece of jewelry, he would sit with infinite patience at his bench, using tools so tiny and delicate that it was difficult to think of them as anything but toys.

It pleased him to read his name next to Brassier's over the shop, and to see some of his best work exhibited in the showcases.

He had designed a brooch for his wife, something very simple, because she did not care for jewelry. An oak leaf and an acorn, its beauty being entirely in the workmanship.

He had handed her the box without a word one evening after dinner.

"What is it?"

"Open it."

She had opened the box and said, without a moment's pause:

"You shouldn't . . . it's far too beautiful . . . It ought to be on display."

"It will be, when you wear it."

"What have I done to deserve it?"

"I just wanted to see you wearing something that I've made with my own hands. As you can see, it's all in white and yellow gold, no colored stones, no diamonds . . ."

Embarrassed, she had murmured:

"Thanks."

She had gone into the bedroom to try the effect in the dressing-table mirror.

"How does it look?"

"Do you like it?"

"Yes."

But, after a few weeks, she had ceased to wear it.

He and the children were gradually growing closer together. He was never home before seven, but often he would find Marlène still at her homework, and would help her when he could.

Admittedly, in some subjects he knew less than she did, having been forced to leave school very young.

She looked like her mother, with the same dark, almost black hair, and brown eyes glittering with little gold flecks.

At fourteen and a half, she was almost a woman, and she liked to talk seriously about things.

"Why don't you ever go out at night, Father?"

"Why should I?"

"Most men like to go out to a café in the evening, don't they? You ought to have more friends, men and women, girl friends if you like. It's not natural to be stuck indoors all the time. It's not as if we were infants, and anyway we've got someone to look after us."

"What if I don't feel like going out?"

"Oh. Well, then, I suppose you're just not like other people."

Another time, when they were alone together, she had said:

"You were very fond of Mother, weren't you?"

"I've never loved any other woman. She was the only person in the world for me, except for you two, of course."

"And did she love you as much?"

"Possibly, but in a different way."

"Why did she go on working after you were married? Did you need the extra income?"

"I was earning enough to keep us both."

The explanation that came first into his mind was:

She wanted to keep her independence. To prove to herself that she was a person in her own right, and not just one half of a marriage partnership.

He had only just realized this, thanks to Marlène. Annette would never have been satisfied with office work. She had needed something more challenging, more arduous, work that would enhance her self-esteem.

But what he actually said to his daughter was:

"She needed to feel that she was doing something useful."

This was also true, but only perhaps as a secondary consideration. As time went by, he began, almost without noticing it, to understand Annette better than when she had been alive—some aspects of her character, at any rate.

He had come to realize that during her lifetime he had been so much under her spell that he had neglected his children.

They, too, felt the change, and began to take a greater interest in his welfare.

When his wife was alive, the whole household had revolved around her.

He shrank from such thoughts, which seemed like an insult to the memory of the dead, almost a blasphemy.

But, on the other hand, was it not in the hope of coming closer to her that he was striving to understand her better?

They had lived together for twenty years, which sounded like a long time. Yet, more and more, he was beginning to feel that their first real meeting, though imminent, had not taken place.

He had scarcely noticed how the years were slipping by. Wrapped up in his own little world, he had taken

64

his happiness for granted. He had been equally happy at home and his workshop, and had never been troubled by doubts.

Jean-Jacques was almost as tall as he was. He stood half a head taller than Nathalie, which she made a great show of resenting. He was one of the star pupils at the Lycée Charlemagne, and was already preparing his *baccalauréat* examinations. Célerin had bought him a motorcycle so that he could enjoy a measure of independence.

He seemed to have no friends, and never brought any of his schoolmates home with him.

"Have you made any plans about your future?"

"No, not yet."

"Well, it's only a matter of months now before you'll have to decide what you want to do."

"I don't want to make up my mind right away. I'd like to spend a year traveling. I'd like to go to England first, to improve my English, then to the United States, and possibly Japan."

In the evenings, Célerin and his daughter and, more often than not, Nathalie watched television in the living room while Jean-Jacques was grinding away at his books. He would sometimes come and sit with them later in the evening, looking dazed after his hours of concentrated work.

Célerin did not censor the programs Marlène was watching. He felt that there was nothing on television about the facts of life that she might not learn equally well from her friends at school.

Unlike her brother, she was careless about her work, doing the bare minimum to enable her to move up each year with her class.

"What does it matter, so long as I don't fail my exams?"

She was in no doubt as to her future.

"I'm going to be an air hostess, or a fashion model."

She was tall and slim. She took great care with her appearance, and used more foundation and nourishing creams, powder, lipstick, and eyeshadow than her mother had ever done.

At the same time, she was entirely without affectation and frank to the point of bluntness. Among other things, she would recount the adventures of some of her friends at school.

"Don't worry . . . I promise I'll let you know when I get to that stage. . . ."

It was disconcerting; at the same time, it flattered him that she should feel able to confide in him.

"Mostly, the girls—the worst of them as a rule—just can't talk to their parents, you know. With you it's different. You're a real friend, and you understand. . . .

A telegram arrived, announcing the death of his father. He drove to Caen, and from there on to his home village.

The old man was almost black in the face. Justine shook her head sagely:

"If I told him once, I told him a hundred times that he mustn't go and lie in the sun after he'd been drinking. I stopped him whenever I could . . ."

They had found him in the field, staring fixedly at the sky. Probably he had felt nothing at all.

"How many years have you been with him?"

"It will be twenty-three years on the Feast of Saint Jean."

"Did he pay you for your work?"

"He never had any money. It was all I could do to make him give me enough to pay the grocer."

"Do you have any family?"

"No one since my husband died."

"What do you intend to do?"

"There's no work for me in the village. I shall go to Caen and find work as a cleaning woman."

"How would you like to stay on here and look after the house as if it were your own?"

"That's not possible."

"Why not?"

"Because you could rent it—and then there are the cows."

"I wouldn't want any rent from you. And you could make a little something for yourself by selling the milk."

She looked at him suspiciously.

"What's in it for you?"

"Nothing. My father owed you a great deal. I just want to make it up to you."

"That's very decent of you. When is the poor man to be buried? And who's to see to it?"

He went to see the carpenter.

"It will have to be good and solid. Old Célerin was no lightweight. I know . . . I helped carry him back to the house. Everything was aboveboard. We called in Doctor Labrousse from the next village."

The day was overcast, with a great deal of low cloud coming in from the sea. He went to see the priest, the key figure in the life of the hamlet.

"Do you remember when you were a kid how you refused to learn your catechism?"

"I remember."

"And now, I daresay, you don't even go to Mass any longer. Your father came to a sad end, but it was only to be expected. Did you know that every Sunday he put on his black suit, a white shirt, and a tie, and came to Mass? But as soon as I went into the pulpit to deliver my sermon, he slunk away to the bistro across the street . . ."

67

The priest was old and he walked with difficulty.

"Would you care for a small glass of Calvados? Don't worry, it's not like that rotgut of your father's."

He filled two tiny glasses from a stone jar.

"This wouldn't hurt a fly."

"What did he die of?"

"I don't know exactly . . . I'm not very familiar with medical jargon. A clot in the brain, someone said. At any rate, he must have died almost instantaneously, so he didn't suffer."

The priest raised a glass to his lips.

"What do you intend to do with the farm?"

"I'm letting Justine have the use of it for her lifetime."

"I'm glad to hear it. She's a decent woman, and she took good care of your father. It's no concern of mine whether there was anything else between them. . . . Are you letting her keep the cows?"

"Yes."

"You're a man of understanding, I can see, Monsieur Célerin. It doesn't seem right to call you Georges, as I used to in the old days. I was told you came here once with your wife. By the way, how is she?"

"She died in an accident."

"I'm very sorry. I shouldn't have asked, but I had no idea."

He arranged for the funeral to take place as soon as possible. On Thursday. Old Célerin's house was not far from the church, and the coffin was hoisted onto a horse-drawn cart. It was draped in a black cloth provided by the priest.

The whole village turned out, and Célerin saw a good many faces he recognized. Most of his schoolmates had left the village, but three or four remained, including the butcher's son, who had taken over from his father.

"How are you?"

"Not too bad. Nothing to gripe about. Except that the village is emptying fast. The old people, like your father, die off, and young ones leave to go to Caen or Paris.

The organ was played by the teacher. He was younger than Célerin. The service left Célerin cold, or, rather, passed over him; he was pondering the inevitability with which one generation succeeds another.

The priest gave a short address. After the benediction, they all went to the churchyard at the back.

His mother was already buried there, and the new coffin was lowered into the same grave.

Everybody filed past and shook hands with him. Now all that was left to do was say good-by to Justine. As he was going out to his car, she said:

"I wonder—please forgive me for bothering you—but don't you think it might be better if I had something in writing?"

He could see that she had a point, and went back into the house.

"Can you give me something to write on?"

She had gone to the trouble of buying an envelope and some cheap, lined paper, the kind that is no longer found anywhere except in remote country places. She also produced a new pen and a bottle of green ink.

"It was the only color they had. My name is Justine-Mélanie Babeuf . . . I am sixty-two years of age."

He wrote out a form of agreement, with the obligations all on his side.

"You really mean that I can stay here for the rest of my life?"

"It's all written down."

She went to get her old steel-framed spectacles, and, mouthing the words under her breath, read through the short document.

"It looks as if that takes care of it. You know more

about these things than I do. Thanks again, anyway. I shall pray for you and your family."

He had spent the whole of his childhood in this dump. He had had a brother and a sister, but both had died in the same year of some infectious ailment—he had never been told what.

It had been his whole world, all he knew, until the stirrings of ambition had prompted him to leave for Paris.

The radio was going full blast when he got back to Boulevard Beaumarchais. It was Marlène. If she had her way, it would be going from morning to night.

"I'm sorry, Father."

For the first few days after Annette's death, he had asked the children not to play the radio or their records, but it would not be fair to expect them to observe the ban forever.

"That's all right. I don't mind."

"How did it go?"

"Very much like any other village funeral."

"Were there a lot of people?"

"Every able-bodied member of the community was there."

"Was your father popular?"

"In his own way. He was the village drunk."

"Is that what he died of?"

"Probably."

"Did you feel very sad?"

"It was sad seeing the old landmarks of my childhood."

"It must be an odd sort of place."

"Not even that."

"All the same, it seems to have knocked you out."

"I saw some of my old school friends, the few who are still living there. I saw the blacksmith, who was as sturdy as an ox the last time I was there. Now he's a white-haired old man hobbling on a stick."

"Poor Father!"

"All I can hope for is that you won't feel the same way if sometime in the future you come back to this apartment. I would like you both to be able to look back with pleasure on your childhood and youth."

"I'm sure we will."

She put her arm through his and kissed his cheek.

"Jean-Jacques is still shut up in his room with his books. He doesn't know you're back."

Nathalie came in from the kitchen.

"I thought I heard your voice. Did everything go off all right?"

"It was rather harrowing."

"Yes . . . there are some places one would prefer never to see again."

Jean-Jacques needed a haircut, and he was drawn about the eyes. He kissed his father on both cheeks.

"I've been grinding like mad. The exams start next week, and it's as well to make sure one has covered the ground. Is dinner ready?"

"I'm just getting the food on the plates," said Nathalie.

"If I were you, I'd take it a bit easier. You're sure to pass."

"One's never really sure."

Célerin was half inclined to agree with his daughter. If there was one thing to be said against Jean-Jacques, it was that he took everything much too seriously, including his work.

"Some of the fellows at school think that when you're young nothing matters. What they don't seem to realize is that our whole future may depend on what use we make of our time in the next few years. What do you think, Father?"

"I agree with you. Nowadays, it's absolutely essential to have the right certificates, even if later one forgets everything one has learned."

Marlène burst out laughing:

"You see!"

Nathalie got up from her usual place at the end of the table and cleared away the soup plates. There was *ravioli* to follow as the main course, which she provided for them once a week. Jean-Jacques made no comment. He was indifferent to food. Marlène protested:

"Again! What day is it? Saturday? I might have known. Every Saturday it's *ravioli!*"

"There's no reason why we shouldn't work out the week's menus together. You'd be sure at least of getting what you liked."

Nathalie was about the same age as his father's servant, Justine, though she looked twenty years younger. She was an extraordinarily good-natured woman, in spite of having been through a good deal of hardship in her time—as they were able to gather from some of the things she had told them.

Instead of becoming embittered, however, she had learned to make the best of things. Everything was a pleasure to her: cooking, cleaning the house, and, when they were younger, taking the children out for walks.

She would never admit to being tired, even when she was spring-cleaning, with a scarf tied around her head —in which she looked even more like a Russian peasant than at other times.

In short, the fact that there was one person missing at the table troubled no one but Célerin. The chairs had been moved slightly wider apart, so that there was now no gap.

Annette had never talked much at mealtimes. She usually seemed somewhat preoccupied, and the faint smile that sometimes lit up her face served rather to mask than to reveal her thoughts.

One question above all tormented Célerin: Had he really succeeded in making her happy?

For twenty years he had simply taken it for granted. The only thing that had puzzled him was her determination to carry on with her work; but in the end he had persuaded himself that it was because she liked to keep busy.

What would she have done with herself, alone in the apartment, while the children were at school? Not only did she not know how to cook; he had never even seen her with a needle in her hand. It was Nathalie who did all the mending, in the evening, by the light of a table lamp in the kitchen.

Although she had watched television with the rest of them, she rarely expressed an opinion.

"What do you think of him, Mother? Do you like his style?"

Marlène was always the one to interrupt the program with her eager questions and comments.

"Not bad."

"I think he's super. All the girls at school have his records. I'd love some for my birthday . . ."

That was how she spent all her pocket money.

Annette had smoked cigarettes in little, short, nervous puffs, grinding them out afterward in the ashtray.

"Do you smoke when you're with your old people?" he had once asked, for no particular reason.

She had frowned, looking for heaven-knows-what hidden meaning in the question.

"I take them cigarettes," she had replied rather drily, "or tobacco for those who smoke a pipe."

He had never been to her office, which was in an annex adjoining Town Hall. She had not suggested it, and he had never ventured to ask.

The whole of that side of her life was a closed book to him. But now he wanted to know everything about her, to feed his memory of her.

The next day, after a great many inquiries, he found his way to a large office with an adjoining anteroom, in which a number of old people were patiently waiting.

A young woman passing through noticed him standing in bewilderment in the middle of the room.

"Can I help you?"

"I am Madame Célerin's husband. I would very much like to talk to the head of her department."

"That's Madame Mamin. I'm sure she'll be pleased to see you as soon as she's free . . . I'll tell her you're here."

4

A woman, hobbling on crutches, came out of the inner office.

"This way, Monsieur Célerin. Madame Mamin will see you now."

The walls were painted a pale green, and the deal furniture was strictly functional. He rather expected to find the occupant raised on a platform, like a teacher.

She was of about the same build as Nathalie, but more compact, courteous in her greeting, though unsmiling.

"So you're our poor little Célerin's husband? Do please sit down."

He had not realized that, during working hours at least, social workers called one another by their surnames.

"I had intended to go to the funeral, but I was told it was to be private. Please accept my sincere condolences, Monsieur Célerin. Your wife was a truly remarkable woman . . . I've trained a good many girls and young women in my time, but never anyone like her. She never complained, however difficult or tiresome the case—indeed she seemed to prefer such cases."

Her face was chalk white, and her eyes gray, unlike Nathalie's, which were brown.

Célerin, a little overawed, could find nothing to say.

He felt out of place here in this office, where the atmosphere was half bureaucratic, half monastic.

Madame Mamin would have made an excellent mother superior, in spite of her well-groomed appearance and her smart silk dress, printed with little flowers.

"I understand she died in a street accident."

"That's right."

"I only heard two days later. I don't read the papers. Where did it happen?"

"On Rue Washington."

"She must have been there on personal business. There's not much call for social workers in that district . . . and besides, it wasn't her area . . ."

"I don't quite understand. What were her working hours?"

He could not have said why he had asked this, except that he was seeking information concerning every aspect of his wife's daily life.

"Social work, by its very nature, cannot be regulated by the clock. Each social worker has her own case load, and it's really up to her how much time she spends with each individual. Your wife, for instance, chose, over and above her normal duties, to undertake housework for the handicapped. . . . And I have a strong suspicion that the little extras she made it her business to provide were paid for out of her own pocket. Would you like to see her office?"

She stood up, and he noticed that she had swollen legs and that she walked with difficulty. She opened a door leading to what he took to be a cloakroom and led him through into another room, also painted green, and furnished with a huge table, at which some ten young women were working.

"They're reading up on the new cases. More come in every day."

76

She pointed to a vacant chair.

"That was Célerin's."

The young women were eying him curiously.

"She never spent much time in the office. She didn't like to keep her 'little old people,' as she called them, waiting."

"What was it that she felt for them? Compassion?"

"Selfless devotion."

He had not the courage to say what was in his mind: that, for his wife, the job had perhaps been a means of escape. Here she had been greatly admired for her devotion to duty, and she was held up as an example to the younger staff.

To the unfortunates whom she visited she had been, in a way, all they had in the world. How they must have looked forward to her coming—the one person who had helped to make their lonely lives tolerable.

"I'm sorry to have disturbed you, ladies."

He returned with Madame Mamin to her office.

"Thank you, Madame Mamin. I knew so little of my wife's activities outside the home. Now I am beginning to understand. Do you have many married women working for you?"

"Very few."

"Any with children?"

"They usually give up when they're expecting their first child."

Annette had not given up. She had devoted herself to the needs of strangers; but, to tell the truth, she had been almost a stranger herself to her own children.

She had lived her real life somewhere other than on Boulevard Beaumarchais, and it was perhaps for that reason that he had so often caught himself watching her with anxiety and bewilderment.

Was it from him that she had been running away?

At times, he had wondered. They had never in all their life together talked frankly, heart to heart.

He had loved her with all his being, and had been humbly grateful to her for taking him as her husband.

Had she not later regretted it, perhaps? Or was it that she was temperamentally unsuited to family life?

It was a warm day, and it was not far to Rue de Sévigné. He decided to walk. As he approached the old building, he quickened his step. Would it not be fair to say that he, too, had his place of refuge? What would have become of him without his workshop and his fellow craftsmen?

"Good morning, Monsieur Georges."

That was their affectionate name for him. Madame Coutance was arranging the jewelry in the showcases, as she did every morning.

The others were already at their benches, bending over their work.

"You're late, boss. That'll cost you a bottle of Beaujolais."

"That's okay by me."

Delighted, Pierrot leaped to his feet and went downstairs to get it.

"How are you getting on with the brooch?"

"With so many stones all of different sizes, getting the settings to fit together is a bit of a problem, but it's coming along."

They were getting more and more work. At the beginning, most of the pieces they made were sold to jewelers, but gradually they had built up good private connections. Rich women, and men looking for a custom-made present, often approached Célerin directly.

Madame Papin was a case in point. She had inherited a huge quantity of old jewelry. The stones and pearls were magnificient, but she considered the settings old-fashioned.

She was over sixty, and there was no elevator in the building; yet she seemed to enjoy her visits to the workshop. In any case, she made sure that they would continue indefinitely by never bringing more than one piece at a time. She looked forward to her chats with Madame Coutance, who was always careful to shut the communicating door as soon as she arrived, as Old Mother Papin would have been quite capable of standing over the craftsmen and telling them how to do their work.

Célerin was working on something for her now. He had done three different drawings before arriving at an austere abstract design, which, although slightly reminiscent of the early 1900's, nevertheless pleased him.

He was making the piece himself because he liked to keep his hand in. He had been working on the white-gold mounting for more than two hours when, at the last minute, he decided to add a contrasting detail or two in yellow-gold wire.

They really could have done with another assistant, but they could not fit in an extra workbench—with the result that they sometimes had to turn work away.

As far as possible, they discouraged customers with conventional tastes:

"You see, madame, the sort of thing you have in mind you could buy ready-made at any first-class jeweler's, and it would cost you less than if we were to make it to order."

Brassier frequently dropped in at some point during the morning.

The jewelers themselves often wanted individually designed pieces.

"I was with Rouland et Fils yesterday. They want a dozen very fine, exclusive pieces, something really original for their show window on Georges Cinq . . ."

"When do they want them?"

"As soon as possible . . . they're always in a hurry, as you well know."

"Do you hear that, guys? It looks as though we'll all be working overtime again."

They always grumbled—purely as a matter of form—Jules Daven especially.

"Do we have a free hand?"

"Subject to the conditions I mentioned. And how about coming to dinner with us one night soon, Georges?"

"You know I don't like to leave the children in the evenings."

It was a rule he had made for himself. Even if his son and daughter were working in their own rooms, he liked to feel that he was there in the apartment and that they were aware of it.

Surely it must make them feel more secure? How else could he make it plain to them that he was there to protect them?

He would watch television or leaf through a magazine. It was always a joy when his daughter came in and sat beside him.

He saw little of Jean-Jacques, who was preoccupied with his forthcoming examinations. Though the boy was only just sixteen, it would not be long now before he left home. He wanted to see something of the world, to learn to stand on his own feet, before settling down to a career.

Annette's death had left a great gap in the household, the greatest gap imaginable. Célerin could not get used to the empty bedroom at night, and sometimes he would catch himself lovingly stroking the sheet on the side where her body had been not so very long ago. Jean-Jacques' departure, though less shocking, would leave yet another gap.

There would be no one left but his daughter. But it was more than likely that she would marry early. In three or four years. It seemed like no time at all. His twenty years with Annette had gone by in a flash.

He would be left alone with the two empty bedrooms. Alone with Nathalie, who would have nothing to do but fuss over him.

It had never struck him before how quickly all these things happen. One took an apartment, planned space for children yet unborn. One furnished their rooms with loving care. One watched them grow up, never realizing that everything one had built up for and around them would be wanted only for a very few years.

"Why are you looking so sad?"

"It's nothing, darling. I was just thinking of your future, yours and Jean-Jacques'."

"Is Jean-Jacques really going to England, and then to America?"

"Yes."

"You don't mind?"

"If that's what he wants, I've no right to stand in his way."

"He's already written to I don't know how many universities for their catalogues . . . apparently, there are special English-language schools in Cambridge. . . ."

His son had done all this without consulting him. He was learning to stand on his own feet, and this was surely cause for congratulation. Nevertheless, Célerin felt a little sad.

"He intends to enroll for the course starting in September, provided he passes his exams—as of course he will."

Suddenly his eyes filled with tears. It was the fifteenth of June already. September was almost upon them. July and August would soon be gone.

He had not yet given a thought to the summer holidays.

"Where would you like to go this summer?"

"What I'd really like would be to spend a couple of weeks in Sables-d'Olonne . . . the parents of one of my friends have a house there, and she's asked me to visit."

"Why have you never brought her home?"

"I don't know. They have a huge apartment on Place des Vosges. Their name is Jourdan. He's a well-known lawyer . . . you may have heard of him. It's great fun there . . . lots going on. There are five brothers and sisters besides Hortense. They've had this house on the beach for years. . . . Hortense has been going there ever since she was a little kid . . . they're very rich. Her eldest brother is eighteen and has his own car . . . as soon as she's old enough to drive, she'll be getting one, too."

His heart contracted. He made a very good living. He and his family wanted for nothing. But he was not "very rich."

He was made aware, for the first time, that children are apt to make comparisons, and not always in their parents' favor.

"You must have heard of him. He's always appearing in sensational cases. The most recent was the Trassin trial . . . you remember, the kidnaping of the Julliard child."

He had a vague recollection of banner headlines in the newspaper.

"He's a fine-looking man—still quite young, graying at the temples, very sexy. He has lots of mistresses."

"How do you know?"

"He makes no secret of it. His wife knows all about it, but it doesn't worry her. He always comes back to her."

"What about the children?"

"The older ones are rather proud of him . . . it's nice being the child of a successful father."

Realizing that this was not perhaps altogether tactful, she hastily added:

"I know I'm proud of the fact that all the most elegant women in Paris are wearing your jewelry."

She took his hand and squeezed it very hard.

"You've got what it takes, you know, Father. I'll just be with them a couple of weeks . . . for the rest of vacation I'm all yours. Where were you thinking of going?"

"What would you say to the Riviera?"

She clapped her hands.

"Saint-Tropez?"

"No . . . a bit too noisy. And besides, we would feel out of place among the sort of people who go there. I was thinking of Porquerolles."

"I've never been on an island."

Jean-Jacques came in in his shirt sleeves, with his collar undone. For several months now he had been shaving regularly.

"What's all the excitement? I could hear you in my room."

"We were talking about the vacations."

"Ah! And what plans have you been cooking up?"

"I'm going to spend two weeks with Hortense in Sables-d'Olonne."

"You mean that fat girl whose father is an attorney?"

"Yes."

"And then?"

"Father thought perhaps Porquerolles."

"Great! I could get in some underwater fishing . . . provided I get through my exams, and someone is prepared to mark the occasion by giving me the necessary equipment!"

"Buy whatever you need, and charge it to me."

Célerin was making up for lost time. At last he was beginning to get to know his children. Until now, his wife had been the only one who mattered. The most he had been able to spare them was an absent-minded kiss and the occasional odd word.

Jean-Jacques turned to his sister:

"Needless to say, you told Father about Cambridge?"

"Shouldn't I have?"

"I would have preferred to tell him myself. I wrote for about a dozen catalogues . . . the best is the six-month course for the Advanced Certificate of Proficiency awarded by the Cambridge University Examinations Board."

"And after that the States?"

"I haven't yet decided where I want to go. The best of the American universities are very hard to get into. Harvard would be my first choice, but, in view of the competition, I can't bank on it. On the West Coast, there's Berkeley, and there's Stanford . . . there's something to be said for both."

Célerin felt he was listening to a voice from another world. He was not being consulted. Well, at least he was being kept informed, which was something.

"What subject do you intend to study?"

"Psychology, I think; possibly sociology."

Was it his mother's career that had put that idea into his head?

"Forgive me, my dears, if I leave you. I'm going to bed. By the way, I shall be gone all of Sunday."

"Where are you going?"

It was they who kept tabs on him. They were used to knowing exactly where he was; so perhaps it was only natural.

"I'm spending the day with the Brassiers. They're having some people in to celebrate the completion of their new swimming pool."

"You lucky thing! I wish I were going swimming."

He kissed them both on the forehead, as he always did.

"Don't stay up too late."

"I've still got about another hour's work."

"Good night to you both."

He went to say good night to Nathalie, who was peeling potatoes for the next day.

"Good night, Monsieur Georges."

This was the most painful moment of the day—opening the door into an empty bedroom, where there was now only one pillow on the bed.

Tonight he felt his loneliness more keenly than ever before. Less than ever did he look forward to spending the day with the Brassiers at Saint-Jean-de-Morteau.

Their relationship had remained cordial, but they had never become really close friends. Célerin, though gratified by his success in life, was humble at heart, and had never forgotten his peasant origins. He was happy as he was, and felt awkward and embarrassed outside his own small social circle.

His children already had a foot on a higher rung of the ladder. Jean-Jacques talked with easy self-assurance of Harvard and Berkeley. When he returned home

85

—if he ever did—he would be a man, a stranger, who would look upon his childhood home as something of a curiosity. Just as he himself had looked upon his father's poky little farmhouse.

Brassier was ambitious. His father had been an ironmonger in Nantes, but Jean-Paul had severed all connections with his past. He was very sure of himself. Presumably he had married Eveline for her looks and style.

For she had nothing else to recommend her. He could see her now, reclining on her couch, with her cigarettes and her records.

Nevertheless, on Sunday morning he set out in his car for Rambouillet. Jean-Jacques planned to work all day. He and Nathalie would be alone for lunch, since Marlène was going to the Jourdans.

This, too, was a kind of breaking up. He was brooding on it altogether too much; and when he was not, it was to Annette that his thoughts invariably returned.

The white villa recalled the houses of Ermenonville. As soon as Célerin got out of the car, he could hear cheerful shouting.

Brassier had said that he was having three or four people in, but there were at least a dozen in the pool, or sitting around it in deck chairs.

"I'm so glad you've come. Later, when things quiet down a bit, there's something I want to discuss with you. Go on, now, and get yourself into bathing trunks."

He had brought his trunks with him, and he changed in the cloakroom. It was too awkward to be introduced to people in a swimming pool, so he simply joined the others in the water. He could only do the breast stroke. Everyone else was doing the crawl. He felt extremely conscious of his spreading waistline, which was the inevitable result of never taking any exercise.

Most of the other guests had already acquired a tan, having just returned from the mountains or the Riviera.

Célerin envied them their self-confidence. They all had it—the young women, even the elderly men, more potbellied than himself but not in the least embarrassed by that or anything else.

He recognized a jeweler with a smart shop on the Champs-Élysées for whom he had made quite a few pieces, but the jeweler did not recognize him.

They were nearly all on first-name terms.

"Whose car did you come in, Harry?"

The voices meshed.

"You're looking too, too marvelous, Marie-Claude!"

"I can't take the credit—I owe it all to my masseur."

Eveline Brassier was the last to put in an appearance. She undulated toward them, wearing the briefest and most revealing of bikinis.

"Hello, everybody. Pay no attention to me. We can all be polite to one another later on."

And, stepping onto the diving board, she executed a flawless dive.

Throughout the day, Célerin felt ill at ease. These people lived in a private world of their own in which there was no place for him. Nor had he any wish to become a part of it.

A bar had been set up on the terrace. One by one, the guests went indoors to get dressed. He was one of the first to do so, conscious that his white skin looked unhealthy next to all those bronzed bodies.

"Champagne? Dry martini?"

A barman in a white coat and white gloves was officiating with an air of supercilious condescension.

The women had changed into brightly colored shorts or diaphanous lounging pajamas. The men mostly wore turtle-neck sweaters. He was the only one in a formal suit.

From time to time, Brassier, taking pity on him, would come over and give him a friendly slap on the back.

"Everything okay? Do ask for anything you want."

Or he would introduce him to someone, who would exchange a few polite nothings and then drift away.

He caught odd snatches of conversation. Horses were a favorite topic. One couple was talking about a recent trip to the Bahamas, and a very young woman was saying, with a show of modesty, that she had just finished writing a novel.

Eveline played the part of hostess to perfection. He could not but admire her self-assurance. She had completely shed her usual languid manner. She was wearing trousers slit to the thighs, with a white halter top knotted under her breasts.

The cocktails and champagne flowed like water. Voices rose a pitch or two. A waiter was weaving his way among the little groups of people, carrying a tray of assorted canapés garnished with caviar, anchovies, and a great variety of cheeses.

Célerin stood morosely apart, wondering what on earth he was doing there.

He did not feel envious of Brassier or his guests, most of whom ignored him.

The dining room was brightly lit. Walls and furniture were white, and the dining table glittered with crystal. Each place was set with four glasses.

The waiter was continually filling them with various wines, the names of which he murmured inaudibly as he poured.

The first course was an immense cold salmon on a

great silver dish, so elaborately decorated that there was a little burst of applause when it was carried in.

It was followed by a whole carcass of lamb that had been roasted on a spit at the bottom of the garden.

He was seated between two women whom he did not know, and he could think of nothing to say to them. One was young, and she engaged in animated conversation with her neighbor on the other side. The other was an elderly woman, the only one there of her age, and she looked almost as lost as he felt.

"Have you known the Brassiers long?" he asked, feeling that he must say something.

She looked at him and smiled. Later, he realized that she was almost stone deaf.

Cigarettes were being taken from gold cases even before the baked Alaska was served, accompanied by still more champagne.

Célerin drank very little, no more than a sip from each glass, yet his cheeks were burning. There were plates of *petits fours* placed at intervals along the table, but no one seemed to want them.

At long last, Eveline gave the sign. She stood up and led them all out onto the terrace. Some stayed there, others went into the garden.

Brassier intercepted Célerin.

"I want you to meet Monsieur Meyer, of Meyer on the Champs-Éysées. You have done so much fine work for him, and you have never met."

"It's a real pleasure to meet you."

It was the man with the enormous stomach and bald head whom he had noticed in the swimming pool. He was wearing a clinging yellow turtle-neck sweater, which outlined breasts that a woman might have envied.

"Monsieur Meyer would like us to have a little talk. The only place where we are not likely to be disturbed is my wife's dressing room."

They went up a staircase with wrought-iron banisters. In passing, Célerin caught sight of a bed covered with a white satin counterpane. White was the dominant color in most of the rooms.

"This way."

The dressing room, however, was not white, but primrose yellow, with Louis Quinze furniture.

"When we built this house, I decided not to have a study because, if I had, I'd be tempted to work in it; I come here for rest and relaxation. Do please sit down . . ."

Both windows were open, and voices reached them from below as a distant murmur.

Monsieur Meyer lit a cigar, going through the pompous ritual with great solemnity.

"Would you care to open the discussion?" he asked Brassier.

"I'd rather leave it to you."

"Very well."

He turned to Célerin.

"I am a very great admirer of your work, and I'm not the only one. My best customers are always interested in anything new of yours. Your work is contemporary. It is in tune with modern fashions. People are getting tired of classic jewelry, in which nothing matters but the stones . . . where the craftsman has merely to produce an unobtrusive setting for a diamond, an emerald, or a ruby. In your work, everything counts. I've seen some lovely things of yours with no stones at all."

He drew voluptuously on his cigar, and a little plume of smoke was momentarily outlined against the blue sky.

"Well, so much for the preliminaries. Now to get down to business. I have a dusty little shop in Deauville, and it's losing money for me. People don't invest in important stones when they're vacationing in Deauville or Cannes or Saint-Tropez. It's my belief that they want something different—in other words, your kind of jewelry.

"As you know, Brassier drops in once a fortnight at my shop on the Champs-Élysées, so we've had every opportunity of talking things over. What I have in mind is to alter the character of the shop in Deauville, to turn it into something quite different from any of my other shops."

Though he had not a single hair on his head, he had bushy eyebrows and hair spouting from his nose and ears. He was thoroughly self-satisfied. Lolling in his chair, he bestowed upon Célerin a look of ineffable condescension.

"In short, I propose that the three of us should form a partnership. Your jewelry will be sold under the name of Brassier et Célerin, which is already well established with my customers. To add the name Meyer would only give rise to confusion.

"My function, in other words, will simply be to put up the capital. The shop will be completely modernized at my expense. I have in mind something very bright and attractive. We'll have two pretty, well-groomed sales girls—or maybe one to start with. You will provide the stock, and the more experimental your designs the better.

"We'll draw up a contract on a fifty-fifty basis, 50

91

per cent for me and 50 per cent to be divided between you two."

"I'm not asking for exclusivity. You will keep your private customers and the other jewelers whom you now supply."

Brassier was watching Célerin somewhat anxiously. The whole idea had apparently come from him.

"What do you say?"

"I don't know . . ." he murmured.

"I won't attempt to press you. But I am a keen businessman—anyone will tell you that—and I've never yet backed a loser. I have a fair idea of your present turnover, and there's no doubt in my mind that you could increase it fourfold in two years . . ."

Brassier hastened to interpose:

"As far as you and I are concerned, naturally we'll split our 50 per cent straight down the middle."

"Our advance publicity will promise the public a unique collection of individually designed, exclusive pieces of jewelry."

Had Célerin at that moment been able to analyze his feelings, he would have realized that, more than anything else, he was embarrassed.

Here were two men who needed him, anxiously hanging on his words, offering him a veritable gold mine.

Because, when all was said and done, these so-called exclusive pieces were his work and his alone. He would often spend five or six days at his drawing board in agonized pursuit of an elusive idea.

He had never been to Deauville; but he knew all about the Maison Meyer on the Champs-Élysées, one of the best-known jewelers in Paris, with branches in London and New York.

"If necessary," said Brassier, "we could take on one or two more assistants."

"And where would we put them?"

"We could always move to larger premises."

No! That was out of the question. He had made his start on Rue de Sévigné, and there he was determined to remain.

"May I instruct my lawyer to draw up a contract?"

Largely through weariness, he yielded. It was not that he despised money. He needed it to pay for his children's education. He had heard that American universities were very expensive places.

"All right," he said with a sinking feeling, "but only on condition that I'm not asked to turn out any mass-produced stuff."

"It's precisely because I want to get away from mass production that I've come to you. I'm looking for a slogan or trade-mark, but I haven't quite hit on it yet . . . something like 'For you alone.'"

"We'll think of something," promised Brassier. "You can go ahead with the contract, Monsieur Meyer, presumably in the form of a partnership agreement. Give me a ring when it's ready, and we'll call in and sign the document."

The fat man could hardly contain his gratification. It was as though he had just acquired a coveted Renoir or Picasso.

"I was about to suggest that we should drink to it . . . I was forgetting I am not in my own house."

He insisted on shaking their hands warmly. Then they went downstairs. Monsieur Meyer posted himself behind a table at which a game of gin rummy was in progress. There were three players, and large sums of money were changing hands.

"May I join you?"

"In a minute or two."

He drew up a chair, and collapsed into it with a sigh

93

of relief. The little transaction upstairs had quite worn him out, it seemed.

"Can you spare me a moment?"

Brassier led his partner away to the end of the garden. Some of the guests were playing bowls. They moved to a secluded spot behind a clump of trees.

"How do you feel about it?"

"I'm not sure yet."

"There's a fortune in it for both of us. And we shan't be giving up our independence. Old Meyer will do well out of it, of course. He's a very shrewd operator . . . I've known him for a long time. But, in the long run, we stand to gain more than he does. As soon as the contract is signed, I'll drive down to Deauville and have a look at the shop, to see how it can be put to the best possible use."

He gave Célerin a friendly pat on the shoulder.

"You'll see . . . you and I will go far . . . Have another think about the workshop. I doubt if you'll be able to manage with only three assistants."

He did not wish to discuss it. He was not feeling any too proud of himself. He could not imagine what had prompted him to say yes, to surrender even a fraction of his independence. He had, in some small measure, sold himself, and it wounded him in his pride as a craftsman.

"I think I'd better be going. Jean-Jacques is alone at home."

"How is he?"

"Working very hard for his *baccalauréat*. In September, he's going to England to study the language."

"For how long?"

"Six months, I think he said. He intends to go to America for his studies, so he'll need to improve his English."

Brassier stared at him in amazement.

"Has he got to that stage already? It seems no time at all since he was just a little kid. He was mad about boats, I remember, and was always building scale models. And Marlène?"

"I daresay she'll be off somewhere, too, as soon as her *baccalauréat* is behind her."

"How time flies!"

"Yes. One tends not to look ahead, not to think of tomorrow until suddenly it's upon one. Please make my excuses to Monsieur Meyer. . . As to your other guests, they don't know me, and they won't miss me."

"Good-by, my dear fellow. Thanks for coming."

His little car was surrounded by expensive sport cars and limousines. Two uniformed chauffeurs touched their caps to him. They were eating cookies, probably brought to them by the cook.

The roads were crowded. The sun was hot. He glanced at the empty seat beside him, where Annette would have been. She had never wanted to learn to drive, making the excuse that she was too absent-minded.

This was true. Whatever she happened to be doing, if one observed her closely one could see that her thoughts were miles away.

Sometimes, Célerin would ask suddenly:

"Where are you wandering?"

She would give a start and blink at him, as though awakened from a dream.

"Why do you say that?"

"Because you seemed to be miles away."

Would Annette have been in favor of the deal he had just concluded? They had seldom discussed business matters. Sometimes, when he tried to describe a design he was working on, she would nod vaguely and say:

95

"Yes . . . yes . . . It sounds very nice . . ."

He felt a sudden upsurge of anger. He had lived with her for twenty years and he had never really known her. Had it been his own fault? Had he been too wrapped up in his work?

Or was it that she, under cover of silence, had had a secret life of her own?

Owing to the traffic, it took him a long time to get back to Paris. It would have been even worse if he had stayed on to the end of the party.

He had no wish to own a country house like Brassier's. He would have been uncomfortable in clothes made to measure by a smart tailor. He had everything he needed for the apartment. The only thing he could think of were good paintings.

He might get a slightly bigger and faster car, just to please his daughter. He intended to devote more time to her from now on. Why shouldn't they go for long drives together on Sundays? They might leave on Saturday afternoon, and stay overnight in some small, pleasant country inn.

It was just a dream. He knew that in reality things would work out quite differently. His daughter, like his son, had her own life to lead, and they would both be happier with friends of their own age.

True, they were fond of him, but he suspected that they thought him odd, a bit of a hermit, out of touch with the realities of life.

Yet, in this, was he so very different from Annette? He had his workshop and his colleagues at their benches. They lived in a small world of their own. They were a family. Annette's family, to which she had devoted herself, had been her old people and her invalids.

He was assailed over and over again by the same

thoughts. They made his head throb, like an attack of migraine.

Why?

If they had lived like any normal couple, they would surely have devoted more time to the children. But they had not been a normal couple. For instance, the only time they gave each other a kiss was first thing in the morning and last thing at night.

Nor had he ever seen his wife in her bath. She had even been reluctant to dress or undress while he was in the room.

He saw her again as she had been that night in the restaurant on the Place des Vosges when she had agreed for the first time to let him take her out to dinner. She had looked very delicate, very fragile.

He remembered the way she had looked at him, with a hint of fear in her large eyes.

He had longed to take her in his arms, to tell her that their life together would be wonderful, to assure her that there was nothing to be afraid of.

Later, she had gained in confidence, but he was sure now that she had never wholly surrendered herself to him. He was her husband. She was fond of him. They had two children who had never given them a moment's anxiety, and they had, by a marvelous stroke of luck, acquired Nathalie, who was a gem, ready and willing to cope with every emergency.

He had to get at the truth, however much it meant rummaging in the past, searching for little meaningful clues.

There was the time, for instance, when she was in the clinic having Jean-Jacques . . . That first day, he had done no more than touch the baby's cheek with the tips of his fingers, and yet he had felt his wife watching him with disapproval.

And indeed, three or four days later, when he had bent down to kiss the baby on the forehead, she had said:

"They're not in favor of kissing babies here."

"Aren't you allowed to kiss him?"

"I'm his mother."

As though the child were not his as much as hers. She had insisted on breast feeding, but behind closed bedroom doors, never in front of him.

What did it mean? She had been the same with Marlène. It was she who had decided on the children's names. She had said quite simply:

"We'll call him Jean-Jacques."

And later:

"We'll call her Marlène."

It was not, he had realized, something to discuss. At the time, this had seemed quite natural. At first, she had devoted herself completely to the children, and seemed made to be the mother of a large family.

But after a few months, she had handed them over to Nathalie and gone back to work.

Not to him, to Nathalie.

Was it that she had not trusted him? Had he failed her in some way?

He found his son in the drawing room, with the record player going full blast.

"Just a second."

He switched it off.

"I suddenly felt I had to relax. Am I glad to see the end of this last fortnight!"

"You'll never have to go through all that again."

"That's what you think. For one thing, depending on which university I decide to go to, I may have to take an entrance exam. And not even in my own language."

"May I ask why you're so keen to take your degree in America?"

"It isn't so much for the academic opportunities. It's that I want to see something of life in a different part of the world. Surely that's an experience worth having for its own sake?"

"Will you come home on the vacations?"

"If you can afford to pay my fare!" he answered with a smile.

"Yesterday, I might have had to say no. But today I concluded a deal that is going to make a big difference to me financially."

"You'll still be independent, I hope, and keep your old workshop?"

Jean-Jacques had been there often as a child. He had been fascinated by all the little tools, and by the view over the rooftops of Paris.

"What a grand place!"

"Yes, son, I shall keep my independence; but all the same I am sharing in a new venture in Deauville, in partnership with one of the biggest jewelers in Paris. We're going to renovate a shop that will sell nothing but exclusive pieces designed by me."

"And Brassier?"

"We shall remain partners, naturally."

"Is he in on the Deauville venture as well?"

"He is."

The boy seemed none too pleased to hear it.

5

Now when he entered the workshop, conversation
ceased abruptly and he was greeted with less familiari-
ty than formerly. It was surely a mark of respect for
him, as a man who had suffered a great misfortune that
others could do nothing to alleviate.

He was conscious of it, but lacked the energy to do
anything about it.

He might, with an effort, have got the conversation
going again, but it was not in his nature to put on an
act.

What, precisely, had crushed him so utterly? If
asked, he might well have said:

"Everything!"

First and foremost, it was his wife's death. He was
constantly conscious of her absence. It began in the
morning when he got up. Annette's toothbrush was still
there, in a glass. Then, when he opened the big
Provençal wardrobe to take out his suit, there on the
left-hand side were all his wife's clothes.

Tentatively, Nathalie had said, after a lapse of several weeks:

"What will you do with them, Monsieur? There are
so many unfortunate women who . . ."

"I want everything left as it is."

Her brush . . . her comb . . . All over the apartment there were countless objects to remind him of Annette.

Marlène, who was much the same build as her mother, had asked if she might have her sweaters, and had been taken aback by his abrupt refusal.

"But why not? It's such a waste . . ."

It seemed to Célerin that as long as his wife's things stayed where they were, some part of her would still be there, in the apartment. From time to time, he would turn his head suddenly, imagining that he had heard her voice.

The recurrent thought that wounded him most keenly was that he had lived with her for twenty years without coming close to her.

Could it be that he was unable to make any woman happy? He had taken it for granted that they loved one another, and left it at that. It had never entered his mind that she might have preferred a different sort of life, or that he could have been more solicitous, more attentive.

He had been wholly wrapped up in his work, as she had been in hers; and in the evenings, when they were at home, they had had nothing to say to one another.

They had been rather like two paying guests in a family boardinghouse—meeting only at mealtimes, eating in silence, and escaping to the television room after dinner.

Did he know his children any better? Jean-Jacques was going away. He was about to enter an entirely different world. He was escaping for good.

What would he remember of his childhood?

And after Marlène, too, had got away, what would she have to remember?

Nothing.

He did not neglect his work. Indeed, he worked harder than ever. He would show them.

His assistants watched him, and whispered among themselves:

"He's had another bad night."

Or else:

"He seems a bit better today."

Brassier dropped in at about ten the day after the pool party. He stopped for a word with Madame Coutance, who was writing out bills, and then came into the workshop. He looked around, assessing the layout.

"You're quite right, you couldn't squeeze another bench in here. I just came by to let you know that I've decided to go to Deauville today. I'm taking Colomel with me . . . he's *the* fashionable interior decorator. We want the shop to be the last word in chic."

Célerin was no longer interested.

"The contract will be ready for signature on Thursday. For my part, I'd rather settle the matter in his office, but Meyer insists that we should all meet for lunch at Tour d'Argent. He's reserved a private room. His lawyer, Maître Blutet, will be along in case of any snags. He thinks our lawyer should be there, too."

"What for?"

"That's what I said."

"There's just one point I'm concerned about. The contract must specify that no mass-produced stuff is to be sold in the shop."

"I've told him that already."

"He agreed?"

"It's as much in his interest as ours. I must be off now. I'm meeting Colomel in a quarter of an hour. We want to get off early."

102

Brassier was back the next day, wild with enthusiasm, and raring to go:

"The shop is just the right size for our purpose. We want to create an atmosphere of intimacy and exclusiveness. It's opposite the Casino, and almost next door to the Normandy Hotel."

The small private room at Tour d'Argent was oak-paneled. The effect was at once austere and luxurious. Monsieur Meyer introduced his lawyer, who turned out to be a young man. He could not have been thirty, but he was very sure of himself.

"Let's have lunch first. A glass of port to start with?"

The port was poured into large glasses from an ancient bottle. Meyer was in high good humor. Once or twice he patted Célerin on the back in a friendly way.

"It gives me pleasure to think that I have been the means of bringing your talent before a wider public."

The lunch had been ordered in advance. They had stuffed lobster to start with while the world-famous *canard au sang* was being prepared.

"What did Colomel say?"

"He's got quite a few ideas already. He promised to let us have some preliminary sketches within the week. The shop will be utterly transformed."

Célerin ate his dessert, wondering what exactly was in it. It was flavored with liqueur, no doubt about it, but what liqueur he could not tell.

"A brandy?"

"No, thank you, I've still got a lot of work ahead of me."

"What about you, Célerin?"

"No, thank you. Not for me either."

Meyer lit a cigar. The waiter cleared the table. The

lawyer went to get his briefcase from the other side of the room.

"Should I read it to you?"

"Yes, please do, slowly. See that everyone has a copy so that they can follow."

The document consisted of five typed folio sheets. " 'This Agreement made between . . .' "

Célerin looking grave, listened attentively. Brassier, who was smoking a cigarette, seemed nervous.

Every contingency that could possibly be foreseen in a partnership of this kind was covered, including a provision that Célerin's life should be insured, with Meyer as beneficiary. There was no such provision with regard to Brassier. He, apparently, was not indispensable.

It was specifically stated that no jewelry from any source other than the workshop on Rue de Sévigné would be exhibited or sold.

"Well! That's it. I hope I haven't overlooked anything. It's my belief that fair shares for all concerned is good business, and it was in that spirit that the contract was drawn up."

"I don't quite understand clause seven," interposed Brassier. "It states that you reserve the sole right to dissolve the partnership, if you so wish, at the end of three years. Why the sole right?"

"Because I am assuming responsibility for all the expenses, and they will be considerable. At the start, for some months—perhaps even for a year—we shall be showing a loss, which I will have to cover. I believe in the project, and I have confidence in you both. But, as in every business venture, there is always a remote chance that we may not succeed.

"I'm willing to give it three years. If, at the end of

that time, the business still shows a loss, I reserve the right to pull out. Then it will be up to you to find another backer."

He drew on his cigar.

"Any other objections?"

"Not as far as I'm concerned," said Brassier.

"No," murmured Célerin, whose attention had wandered.

The lawyer took a gold fountain pen from his pocket and handed it to Meyer, together with the four copies of the contract.

"Sign here . . ."

"It's not the first contract I've signed, you know . . ."

Brassier was the next to sign the four copies, and finally Célerin.

Meyer must have pressed a buzzer concealed under the carpet, for, as if by magic, a waiter appeared with a bottle of 1929 champagne.

"That's the way to do business, Monsieur Célerin. Last Sunday morning you and I hadn't even met, and now, for better or worse, we are partners."

He burst into a loud laugh.

"To our new company!"

In a spirit of recklessness, or for some other obscure reason, Célerin drank three glasses of champagne in quick succession. As he had already had port as an *apéritif* and wine with his meal, his head was swimming.

Abruptly, he got to his feet and left, without a word to anyone. His black mood had returned. What would Annette have thought, had she been there, of all the pomp and ceremony—and what would she have thought of him in the state he was in? He stumbled along the street, scarcely knowing where he was. He was not far from Rue de Sévigné. He had been a sober man all his life. He could not remember a single occasion when he had been drunk.

At the corner of Quai de la Tournelle, he went into a bistro, although his legs felt as if they were made of cotton wool.

"A double brandy."

Leaning on the counter, he could see his reflection in the mirror behind the bottles. The proprietor was in his shirt sleeves and wearing a blue apron. The only other living creature in the place was a ginger cat, which came over and rubbed itself against his legs.

"Well!" he mumbled. "Here's someone who takes an interest in me, anyway."

Then he looked again at his reflection in the mirror. The proprietor, who knew the signs, teased him good-humoredly.

"That's not your first today, is it?"

"My first what?"

"Your first brandy."

"Well, there, you see, that's where you're wrong. I've had Pommery '29 . . . three glasses. No, four. And before that, Chambertin . . . and before the Chambertin . . . I can't remember . . ."

"Do you mean to say you've just come from the Tour d'Argent?"

"Absolutely correct. Lunch in a private room . . . I think I'm beginning to get drunk . . . I should have got drunk before this, when my wife died, but it never occurred to me. . . . Another . . ."

"Is that wise?"

"Don't worry . . . I won't make any trouble . . . I'm an inoffensive sort of man . . . d'you hear me? Inoffensive . . ."

And he put his tongue out at his reflection in the mirror

He lit a cigarette with difficulty, his hands were shaking so badly.

"I live across the river on the Boulevard Beaumarchais, but I'm not going home right now. I'll have to look in at the workshop first. I'm needed there. . . . They're a splendid lot . . . you won't find better goldsmiths anywhere in Paris."

"Are you a goldsmith?"

"Yes, monsieur. And, as from today, I have my own shop. And guess where my shop is."

"I don't know."

"In Deauville. I've never been to Deauville, but I'm told it's where all the best people go."

He was talking on and on to prevent himself from bursting into tears.

"How much?"

"Three francs eighty."

He fumbled in his pockets, found some loose change, and paid.

On his way out, he called back:

"You're a very decent fellow."

He crossed the Seine, carefully avoiding oncoming cars.

"One accident in the family is quite enough."

Then he sniggered:

"Meyer won't have had time to take out that insurance policy yet!"

Meyer had a nerve to insure against anything happening to him!

"I must remember to find out what I'm worth on the open market."

If only he could get rid of his black thoughts. He

could not bring back his wife. She was dead. Everyone died, sooner or later. She was buried in Ivry Cemetery; he had chosen a suitable headstone that would later mark her grave. One day, he would join her there.

As for the children, he was always thinking of their welfare. Had they ever given a thought to his? Yes! Jean-Jacques had advised him to remarry, as though there were something shameful in being a widower.

And what if he preferred to remain a widower?

He found himself at Town Hall, where he had recently seen Madame Mamin. She was the boss. She had the right build for it. Annette must have been one of her favorites. Everyone had loved Annette. She was universally regarded with a kind of protective affection. She had had such an abundance of energy, in spite of her frail appearance. She had never thought of herself, only of others.

And what of him? What impression did he make on people? He was virtually ignored, except for his buddies in the workshop and Nathalie.

Nathalie, surely, was very fond of him. But she was growing old. She would not be able to work very much longer. What would he do then? And when she died . . . ?

These were matters that he could not face when he was sober. In time he would be not only a widower, but an old widower, tottering to the local shops to buy just enough food for one.

Eventually, he got to Rue de Sévigné. Slowly, he went up the stairs, holding on to the banister. Madame Coutance stared at him in amazement. He had had too much to drink, that was obvious.

"Come into the workshop. I have important news for you all."

Looking thoroughly uncomfortable, she followed him

in. Some people can get drunk with impunity; others can't.

They had never seen him drunk before, and now he could hardly keep on his feet.

"Well, here it is, folks. It's settled, and it concerns all of you. I, and Brassier, too, of course, have just concluded an extremely important deal, all signed, sealed, and delivered.

"As soon as the alterations are completed, we shall have our own shop in Deauville, right opposite the Casino . . . a shop devoted exclusively to the sale of jewelry designed and made in this workshop."

They all stared at him, not knowing whether to laugh or cry.

"We are now partners of Meyer, I mean as regards the shop in Deauville, of course, not the one on the Champs-Élysées. Well, aren't you going to congratulate me?"

"How are we going to cope with the extra work? Will you be taking on more staff?"

"Where would we put them?"

Suspiciously, Jules Daven asked:

"You're not thinking of moving from here?"

"Over my dead body! This is where I started, and here I intend to stay until I die."

To Pierrot he said:

"Get us a couple of bottles of wine . . . something good."

The men exchanged looks of consternation. They did not know what to think. They could not help worrying over the state Célerin was in; they were much too fond of him.

"Is it really true about Deauville?"

"Where do you think I had lunch? At the Tour d'Argent. And after the meal, the lawyer read out the contract to us, and we all three signed it. . . . I'm afraid we shall have to put in some extra overtime now and again . . . but I may as well tell you that, beginning next month, you'll all be getting a raise."

"What will Monsieur Brassier have to say about it?"

"Monsieur Brassier will have nothing to say. Whose life is being insured for the benefit of Monsieur Meyer, his or mine? Mine is, because without my work . . ."

His eyes were streaming with tears.

"What a fool I am! I've had too much to drink. I know very well I've had too much to drink, and that I'm babbling on like a soak . . ."

"Shall I make you some coffee?" suggested Madame Coutance.

"It would only make me sick. Oh! what the hell . . . having got this far, I might as well go the whole hog . . . Daven, if, when it's time to leave, I can't walk straight, please take me home in a taxi."

Pierrot returned with the wine, and the others watched Célerin with growing anxiety. He intended to go on drinking, they could see. And he did.

"Your very good health . . . Here's to the success of our new shop"

With a feeling of sadness, they all raised their glasses.

"From now on, we'll be working like crazy to build up a stock for the opening of the shop."

The buzzer sounded. The communicating door was open. Célerin exclaimed:

"Well, if it isn't Old Mother Papin!"

"Madame Veuve Papin," she corrected him.

Madame Coutance attempted to get between him and the door, but he pushed her aside.

"Do you go to Deauville for the summer?"

"I have a villa just outside the town . . ."

"Well, next time you go, you'll see a shop selling nothing but jewelry made by us."

"Do you mean you're closing this shop?"

"Absolutely not! Look, do come in and have a drink with us. It's this new venture that we're celebrating."

Madame Coutance shook her head and shrugged helplessly.

"Don't worry. It's a good wine."

She took a mouthful, and choked on it.

"What have you brought us today?"

She looked at Madame Coutance, as though seeking guidance. The saleswoman responded with a slight inclination of the head.

"An emerald. It came out of a very old necklace. My aunt must have inherited it from her mother or grandmother."

From her bag, she produced a magnificent emerald wrapped in tissue paper.

"What do you want done with it?"

"It's too big for a ring. I thought perhaps a brooch."

"Just a minute . . . No, stay where you are. You shall have your design right away."

He reeled over to his drawing board, set up a sheet of paper, and traced the outline of the stone.

"You want something modern, I presume?"

He took up his pencil and began what looked like a senseless jumble of lines, pausing briefly to fill his glass and empty it at a gulp.

"Now, just wait, and don't worry. . . . I may be drunk, but my mind is clear. That sounds crazy, doesn't it? Nevertheless, it's true.

"These fine lines here represent blades of grass. Here, give me the stone."

He placed it in the center of the sketch.

"Naturally, this is no more than a rough outline.

111

What I have in mind is a little nest—stylized, of course —with your wonderful green emerald set deep in the heart of it."

They all gathered around, fascinated. In a couple of minutes, under their very eyes, Célerin had created a ravishing jewel, as fine as anything he had ever done.

Jules Daven took him home in a taxi, since he was quite incapable of getting there on his own. Célerin managed to get the key out of his pocket, but could not focus to fit it in the lock.

"Well, here you are, then. If you'll take my advice, you'll go straight to bed and stay there for the whole of tomorrow. *Au revoir*, my dear fellow."

Daven was the only one who used the informal *"tu"* with him. They had been colleagues on Rue Saint-Honoré, and Daven, who was now fifty-four, was his senior by several years.

Célerin held him back by the coat sleeve.

"Don't go yet. Listen to me . . . You must let me get you a drink . . . Yes! I insist . . . This is a great day in our lives, don't forget, a memorable day"

He was delighted to find that he could still pronounce the word "memorable," and he smiled as he said it.

Nathalie came in. Grasping him by the arm, she signaled to Daven that he could go.

"Come along," she said. "I'll get you a drink if you want one. But your friend is drunk already. He shouldn't have any more."

"Daven?" he exclaimed in bewilderment.

"I don't know his name, but he's very unsteady on his feet."

The children were in their rooms, doing their homework. She guided Célerin into his bedroom.

"You stay here. I'll bring you a glass of wine right away."

112

She was as good as her word. He had not moved. He just stood there, dazed.

"Won't you drink with me?"

"Wine doesn't agree with me, as you very well know."

"Did you hear that word I used?"

"Which one?"

"Memorable. This is a memorable day. I've had lunch at Tour d'Argent, and I have signed a contract."

"Let me help you off with your coat."

He leaped from one idea to another.

"Tell me, Nathalie . . . you're a friend . . . the best friend I've got, and I don't know what I'd do without you . . . You were my wife's friend, too . . . she must have confided in you from time to time . . ."

She loosened his tie, and sat him down on the bed. He was as docile as a little child.

"Do you think she loved me? . . . I mean really and truly loved me, if you know what I mean?"

"I'm sure she did . . ."

"You're only saying that to please me. I'm nothing but a peasant. I grew up in a sort of pigsty . . . I had no education to speak of . . . But she was a woman of great refinement . . . that's the only word for it . . . refinement."

He caught sight of his glass, still half full, on the beside table.

"Would you hand it to me, please?"

He drained it. Nathalie had great difficulty in getting him into his pajamas. He was a dead weight, and he gave her no assistance.

"You go to sleep now. If you need anything, call me."

"Where are the children?"

"In their bedrooms, working."

113

"I couldn't face them, like this . . ."

"You won't have to. Go to sleep."

Scarcely had he closed his eyes than he was snoring, his mouth wide open. Nathalie tiptoed from the room.

Nathalie concocted a story for Jean-Jacques and Marlène: their father had come home early, feeling unwell—it was probably the beginning of tonsilitis—and he had gone straight to bed.

"Be very quiet. We mustn't disturb his rest."

Twice in the night, she looked in to satisfy herself that all was well, and both times she found him in a deep sleep.

It was total oblivion, without dreams. From time to time, he turned over heavily, making the bedsprings creak.

At six o'clock, he woke as usual and, opening his eyes, saw streaks of sunlight through the slats of the Venetian blinds. He sat up. It was when his feet touched the floor that he became aware that he had the most frightful headache. He had never experienced anything like it.

His eyes were smarting as well, and his mind was in turmoil. He looked thoughtfully down at his pajamas. He had no recollection of having undressed, still less of putting on his night clothes.

He stood up dizzily, and lurched into the bathroom. He was alarmed at what he saw reflected in the mirror. His stomach was heaving, but although he bent over the toilet bowl, retching, he could not bring anything up.

There was a bottle of aspirin in the medicine cupboard. He swallowed three tablets with a glass of water, and nearly choked on them.

He had been drinking brandy. There was still a slight aftertaste of it, he thought, at the back of his throat.

114

But where had he been when he drank it? This was still a mystery.

He was swaying on his feet. He had better get back into bed. He fell asleep again almost at once. When he next woke, the hands of the alarm clock stood at ten. He went to the door in his bare feet and opened it a crack.

"Nathalie!" he shouted. "Nathalie!"

Seeing that she did not immediately come running, he felt let down, miserable.

"Memorable."

What on earth had made him say that? Apart from getting disgustingly drunk, what had he done that could be described as memorable?

By the time Nathalie appeared, he was back in bed. She looked very fresh in her checked cotton apron, with the scarf that she always wore tied round her head when she was doing the housework.

"How do you feel?"

"Rotten . . . I'm ashamed . . ."

"If everyone who took a drop too much once in a while was to be ashamed of it, this world could indeed be called a Vale of Tears."

"Who put me to bed, Nathalie?"

"I did."

"Did the children see me?"

"They didn't even put their heads in at the door. I told them you thought you might be getting tonsilitis, and had thought it best to go straight to bed."

"Could you bring me a cup of strong black coffee?"

"It's filtering through now. As soon as I heard you call, I poured on the boiling water."

He was sitting up in bed, propped against his pillows, his hair in disarray. He was docile, like a good little boy, waiting for Nathalie to come back and cosset him.

"Watch out. It's very hot."

"Have you been out shopping yet?"

"I telephoned my order to the butcher, and he's already delivered the meat. And there are some vegetables left over from yesterday."

"You were afraid to go out and leave me, is that it?"

"You might have needed something."

"I must have made a disgusting spectacle of myself last night."

"Not at all. You behaved very well."

"What did I say?"

"You told me about the contract you had just signed."

"I didn't make that up. I really have signed a contract, a very important one. I'm beginning to wonder whether it was the right thing to do. It was Brassier who talked me into it."

"I do hope, at least, that you haven't signed away your workshop."

She disliked Brassier. She thought him too ambitious. And she could not stand Eveline.

She had said of her:

"That sort of woman thinks of nothing but clothes and beauty care. In ten years' time, you may be sure, she'll be thinking about a face lift. And what does she find to do with herself all day?"

"No. I haven't sold the workshop—quite the reverse . . . Just a minute . . . let me think . . . I believe . . . yes, that's it . . . One of our best customers came into the shop while I was there . . . I don't know what she must have thought . . . I hope I didn't say anything foolish . . ."

The coffee had done him good.

"May I have another cup?"

He asked for it so humbly that she could not help

116

smiling. She felt an upsurge of affection for this great baby who had done a foolish thing and was almost begging to be forgiven.

He dialed the number of the shop on Rue de Sévigné.

"Hello! Madame Coutance? Will you put me through to Daven, please."

He heard footsteps receding and returning.

"Hallo!"

"Jules? Sorry to bother you . . . I don't think I'll be coming in this morning."

"That's a surprise!"

"I got very drunk, didn't I?"

"That's an understatement."

"Tell me, did I do or say anything foolish?"

"Not a thing."

"I have a vague recollection of Madame Papin . . ."

"You hailed her as 'Old Mother Papin,' but you managed to put it right."

"What did I say to her?"

"You told her that you were opening a shop in Deauville, but not to worry; that you would continue to work here and take care of your old customers as before."

"I don't remember a thing about it."

"There's better to come . . . listen to this. She brought in an emerald of about twenty carats that had belonged to her aunt's grandmother or great-grandmother. She asked if you could set it in a brooch. . . .

"You looked at the stone for a bit. Then you went over to your drawing board, and did what looked at first like a scrawl. Less than five minutes later you put the stone in the middle, and it was a revelation. You've never designed anything so beautiful, I can assure you."

"You're quite sure I didn't make a nuisance of myself? At best, I must have looked an awful fool."

117

"I assure you, you didn't. You were as good as gold. I put you in a taxi and took you home. You kept saying you wanted one last brandy."

"I know I had several brandies, but I can't remember where."

"I don't know either. When you got here you sent out for two bottles of first-rate wine."

"What did they say?"

"Who?"

"The boys."

"Nothing. They were a bit shaken. They'd never seen you in such a state before . . . and they were afraid that you might be thinking of cutting loose and going to settle in Deauville . . . you see, you kept talking about this terrific deal you'd pulled off, something to do with a shop in Deauville"

"That's right. We are going to have a shop there, but we'll still be doing all the work in Paris. . . . Thanks, old man. Please apologize to them all on my behalf, and that includes Madame Coutance"

Standing over him with her hands folded on her stomach, Nathalie watched him drink his second cup of coffee. It tasted less bitter to him than the first.

"I suppose I talked a blue streak last night?"

"You did."

"I haven't the faintest recollection of anything I said. The last thing I remember was sending out the apprentice to get a couple of bottles of choice wine."

"I think you'll find, in the long run, that it's done you more good than harm."

"How do you mean?"

"You've been under a severe strain for weeks, and bottling it all up."

"I kept thinking about Annette."

118

"And so you always will, but it will no longer be an obsession."

"I don't think I treated her right . . ."

"What do you mean?"

"I've thought about it a lot. A woman needs affection, and all the little attentions that go with it. I took things too much for granted. Starting from the assumption that we loved one another and always would, it never occurred to me that it was necessary for me to go on telling her so. She was very sensitive, with great delicacy of feeling, and all the time I lived with her I never noticed . . ."

"On the contrary, you were always most loving and considerate."

"Not loving enough. And now I'm eaten up with remorse."

"There's no need. She had her own professional life, which was what she wanted, and, if I may be permitted to say so, she was of a stronger character than you are . . . By the way, what have you decided about her clothes?"

He had, at last, to face the fact that they could not be left in the wardrobe indefinitely. It was a fresh shock every morning to see them hanging there like sloughed skins. To stuff them into a trunk and carry them up to the attic would be worse still . . . like a second burial.

"Do you know anyone who could make use of them?"

"There's a widow I meet sometimes in the shops. She's a brave little thing with two small children. I don't know her address, but I could get it from the butcher."

"Do that. Give her all Annette's things."

But for the fact that he had been drunk the previous night, he would probably not have found the courage to

119

come to this decision. His headache was becoming less severe, though he still had a queasy stomach.

One last objection occurred to him:

"Supposing I were to see her in the street wearing a dress of my wife's?"

"You couldn't be sure it was hers. Madame bought her clothes ready-made, not from an exclusive dressmaker."

He acknowledged that this was so.

It had done him good to talk to Nathalie. He had kept things to himself far too long.

"You know . . . she was my world."

"I've always known that."

"For her it wasn't quite the same. She was my wife. . . . She gave me the affection that a wife is supposed to give her husband . . . no more. Am I right?"

"I can't say, because how can you tell what goes on in another person's heart and mind. She was very much wrapped up in her work, don't forget . . . she might have been one of the Little Sisters of the Poor."

"Do the children talk about her?"

"Rarely. Sometimes—for instance, when I cook them spaghetti—one of them will say:

" 'Mother was the one who adored spaghetti.' "

"Did you know that we shall soon be losing Jean-Jacques?"

"He did mention it a couple of weeks back."

"Has he ever talked to you about his mother?"

"I don't think so. They weren't very close. I was the one he used to come to with his secrets."

"In a few years time it will be Marlène's turn to leave home, and then there will only be the two of us left."

"By that time I'll probably be walking on crutches, or at least need a cane.

"You can train a girl to help you with the heavy work."

"If you think I'd put up with having some wretched girl under my feet! Either I carry on as I am, or I retire to an old people's home."

He was suddenly in tears, unable to stop himself. Was it just all part of his hangover?

She watched him in silence. It was a relief to him. It was soon over. With his face hidden in his hands, he asked for a handkerchief. She brought him one, and then handed him a washcloth soaked in cold water.

"Put this on your forehead."

He had always thought of himself as a strong man, and yet, weeks after his wife's death, he had still not regained his self-control.

"I've been behaving like a child."

"I'll run you a bath. Have a long soak, and don't forget to shave—that is, if you can manage to hold the razor."

"Are my hands shaking all that much?"

"A bit. It's only to be expected."

"Was it here that I drank all that brandy?"

"All I gave you was one glass of wine. If I'd refused, you would probably have lost your temper, and the children were in their rooms."

She turned on the faucets. He listened to the familiar and reassuring sound of running water.

"While you're in the bath, I'll start the vegetables."

"What time is it?"

"Nearly eleven. Put on something light. It's very warm today. I don't think you need spend the whole day in bed. It would do you good to go to work for a few hours."

"You may be right."

He felt like seizing her hand and kissing it. She went into the bathroom and turned off the faucets.

"Stand up for a minute and let me see what shape you're in."

She said it banteringly, but she meant it. He got up, and walked to the window and back.

"Well, did I pass the test?"

"Yes . . . you can manage on your own."

He brushed his teeth vigorously, in the hope of getting rid of the hateful taste in his mouth. Then, taking off his pajamas, he lay down in the bath.

He shaved more carefully than usual, and dressed in one of his favorite suits, with a cheerful tie. He was anxious that the children should see him looking his best.

Marlène came in first.

"Oh! So you're up!"

"It was a false alarm. I had a sore throat yesterday afternoon, and I thought it might develop into tonsilitis."

"Say, you look elegant! Whom are you going to see?"

"Just my friends at the shop."

Jean-Jacques, in his turn, exclaimed:

"Not in bed?"

"As you see, I'm disgustingly healthy, as usual."

It was true. The children had never known him to spend a whole day in bed.

He had a glass of red wine with his lunch, and it make him feel better.

"How's the work going?"

"Only three days to the exams."

"You'll breeze through them, I'm sure."

"I wish I were as confident as you are . . . they're making them stiffer all the time."

He looked about him in the street, with its patches of

sun and shade, as though he had not been out of doors for a long time. He knew nothing of the people rubbing shoulders with him on the sidewalk or crossing his path, and yet he watched them with interest. They were all human beings with human failings, and possibly also reserves of human courage.

He greeted Madame Coutance with a cheerful "Good afternoon!"

She had lost her husband after only three years of marriage. He had been an army officer. As he was riding in a forest, he was thrown off his horse by the branch of a tree.

She had decided to go out to work, and, little by little, her confidence and good humor had been restored.

"Hallo, everyone!" he said, as he came into the workshop.

Suddenly, he caught sight of the sketch he had made on the previous day. Daven had not lied to him. It was the best thing he had ever done.

6

_____

He was alone in the living room, ostensibly watching television, but in fact pursuing his own throughts, when he felt someone move beside him. It was Marlène, who had crept, unnoticed, into the room.

Shyly, she put her hand on his, and murmured:

"I do hope you won't be lonely when I'm staying with my friend. I do look forward just as much to being with you in Porquerolles."

There was silence while a posse of cowboys hurtled across the screen.

"How about Jean-Jacques—is he coming, too?"

"I don't know. We haven't discussed his vacation plans yet. I want him to feel free to do whatever he likes . . . he must have friends of his own . . ."

"You are an angel, Father!"

And she gave him a resounding kiss on the cheek.

Surely she and Jean-Jacques had noticed the grief that had weighed upon him since their mother's death, and would have expressed their sympathy had they not been inhibited by an innate reserve.

He slept better that night. In the morning he noticed that Annette's clothes had been removed from the wardrobe and the chest of drawers. He wondered if he had been right to follow Nathalie's advice.

As usual, he had his breakfast alone. He was always the first to leave the house. At the corner of Boulevard Beaumarchais, he almost collided with a policeman in uniform. As he turned around, he saw that it was Sergeant Fernaud, the officer who had brought the news of his loss. At the same moment the sergeant also looked back.

"You're a long way from your beat, aren't you?" Célerin said, smiling.

"True enough. I'm here on private business, not on duty."

The sergeant looked at him searchingly.

"How are you doing?"

"As well as can be expected."

Fernaud hesitated, then came out with what was on his mind.

"Did you go to Rue Washington?"

"What for?"

The sergeant seemed to regret his question.

"I don't know . . . Perhaps to find out where your wife had been . . ."

"Are you quite sure she was coming out of a house in that street?"

"Well, at any rate, there are two witnesses who claim to have seen her."

"Has there been an official inquiry?"

Célerin was beginning to suspect that the sergeant knew more than he had told him.

"It's no business of ours where she had been. Our inquiries were concerned only with the accident itself."

Célerin's anxious, even suspicious manner made him feel uneasy. Hastily, he shook him by the hand.

"If you'll excuse me, I must get back to Place de la Bastille."

There was nothing he could put his finger on. The man had simply asked him a question, but it was a question that disturbed Célerin. Perhaps he ought to have had a word with the witnesses himself. The sergeant had seemed surprised to learn that he had not done so.

In the workshop on Rue de Sévigné, they were all at their benches already. Jules Daven was absorbed in assembling the delicate components of the widow Papin's brooch.

"Anything new?"

"Nothing. Everything's fine."

"I shall have to be out for a time this morning."

He said it with regret. He was not looking forward to what he was about to do. He felt it was a kind of betrayal of Annette.

He did not have his car with him. He seldom took it to work. It was no distance from the apartment.

He got on a bus. It was a warm day. The sun was shining, and already there were a few people sitting on the café terraces.

He got off at Avenue Georges Cinq. At the corner of Rue Washington, he almost turned back. Something told him he was trespassing. Annette had earned the right to be left in peace.

All the same, he walked on until he came to a yellow-fronted greengrocer's shop, with the name "Gino Manotti" painted above it.

The greengrocer and his wife were inside the shop emptying a crate of grapefruit.

"What can I do for you?"

He had a strong Italian accent, and the bluish-tinted black hair typical of Mediterranean stock.

"My name is Georges Célerin."

"What name did you say?"

"Georges Célerin."

"Are you a salesman?"

"No. I am the husband of the woman who was run over by a truck just outside your door."

"I remember."

He turned to his wife and said something to her in Italian.

"It was terrible—almost as though she had thrown herself under the wheels of the truck on purpose . . . but of course she didn't. The road was wet, and she slipped."

"Where had she come from?"

"One of the houses."

"Which one?"

"I still think it was number forty-seven. Someone else who was out there in the street swears it was number forty-nine . . ."

"Had you ever seen her before?"

"Well, you know how it is. We see so many people . . ."

"I'm much obliged to you."

As he did not know the name and address of the other witness, he called in at the police station on Rue du Faubourg-Saint-Honoré.

There were several people sitting on a bench, waiting their turn. He was about to join them when a policeman posted near the staircase called him over.

"Can I help you?"

"My name is Georges Célerin."

The policeman frowned, as though the name meant something to him but he could not remember what.

"I am the husband of the woman who was run over by a furniture truck on Rue Washington."

"Ah, yes, I remember now . . . Sergeant Fernaud was on the case. He isn't in at the moment."

"I know . . . I ran into him a few minutes ago."

"What is it you want?"

"I've seen Gino Manotti, the greengrocer . . ."

"He's a decent fellow."

"I wonder if you could tell me the name and address of the other witness, the cne who was passing by at the time of the accident?"

The policeman looked at him very much as Sergeant Fernaud had done a short while ago.

"I'll have to look up the file. There's no one to relieve me at the moment. If you could come back in half an hour . . ."

He walked the streets. He could think of nothing else to do. Then he went into a bar and had a cup of coffee.

He was becoming hypersensitive. It needed only a glint in someone's eye or a furrowed brow to arouse his suspicions.

The half hour seemed interminable. He had time to loiter in front of at least twenty shopwindows. He could almost have made an inventory of the goods displayed.

When he got back to the police station, the officer to whom he had spoken handed him a sheet of paper with the name and address:

Gérard Verne
Representative, Belor Oil Company
Avenue Jean-Jaurès
Issy-les-Moulineaux

He went by Métro and, having asked the way, had no difficulty in finding the apartment occupied by the representative of the Belor Oil Company. He went up to the third floor. The concierge was sweeping the stairs, and from the apartments came the sounds of women doing their housework.

He rang the bell; the door was opened by a woman in a housecoat and bedroom slippers.

"What do you want?"

128

"Is Monsieur Verne at home?"

"He is, but he's in bed with flu."

"I wonder if I might have a word with him?"

"Are you a company inspector?"

"No."

"You're not the doctor, are you?"

She was evidently suspicious of him.

"I'll go and see if he's awake."

She was back in a few seconds.

"I'm sorry about the mess. I haven't finished cleaning in there."

She led him to a small room, where a man with at least two days' growth of stubble was lying in bed. He raised himself into a sitting position against the pillows, at the same time inspecting his visitor with interest.

"I've never seen you before, have I?"

"No. But you have seen my wife."

"What do you mean?"

"You were a witness to an accident on Rue Washington."

"That's correct. Who are you?"

"The husband of the woman who was killed."

"What is it you want to know?"

"Did you really see my wife coming out of one of the houses?"

"Isn't it a bit late in the day to ask me that?"

"Did you see her?"

"As clearly as I see you. Afterward, I even made a note of the number of the house. It was number forty-nine. There were two brass plates to the left of the door, one of them a doctor's. But I've already told all this to the police . . ."

"Was she running?"

"Not running, exactly. She was walking very fast, as

if she were in a hurry. Then, suddenly, she darted out into the road. It was pouring rain. She slipped and fell right under the wheels of the truck."

"You're quite sure she was coming out of the building?"

"Quite sure. I'm an observant sort of person."

"Thank you very much. Please forgive my disturbing you."

He took the Métro back to Avenue Georges Cinq. It was true that he might have made inquiries sooner. If he had not done so, it was out of respect for his wife's privacy. He had never, in twenty years of marriage, so much as opened one of her personal drawers.

He went first to number forty-seven, and was fortunate enough to find the concierge in the lodge. As always, he had a photograph of Annette in his wallet.

There was a delicious smell of simmering stew in the lodge. The concierge was young and pleasant-looking.

"If it's about an apartment . . ."

"No."

He held out the photograph.

"Have you ever seen this woman?"

She examined it carefully, then took it over to the window for a closer look.

"She reminds me of someone, even to the little white collar . . . Isn't she the lady who was killed near here in an accident?"

"Yes. I wondered if she'd been to see one of your tenants."

"Not to my knowledge, and I doubt if anyone could get in here without my seeing them—especially in the afternoon, when I'm always in here with my sewing."

"I'm much obliged. Forgive me."

He was forever apologizing. He had always been shy, no doubt on account of his childhood background.

130

The apartments next door were luxurious. The concierge was upstairs, and he stood waiting outside the glass door of the lodge for quite a time. Eventually, she came down the stairs carrying a pail and mop.

"What is it?"

She was somewhat older than the concierge in number forty-seven, and her small eyes were mistrustful.

"My name is Célerin."

It never occurred to him that anyone might be ignorant of the details of the accident or the name of the victim.

"And what is that supposed to mean?"

Opening the door of the lodge, she called back over her shoulder:

"Wait there while I get rid of this nut!"

A big black cat, which had been curled up in a chair with a velvet cushion, leaped to the floor, arched its back, and came and rubbed itself against Célerin's legs.

"Come in, and tell me just what it is you're after. I take it you're not trying to sell vacuum cleaners or encyclopaedias? And if it's the fortuneteller on the fifth floor you want, she died almost a year ago . . . which doesn't keep people from asking for her, even after all this time . . ."

Feeling sick at heart, he held out the photograph.

"Do you know this person?"

She looked up sharply, and her eyes were intent.

"Are you her husband?"

"Yes."

She hesitated perceptibly.

"Have you been to the police?"

"Yes, and if necessary I shall go back to them."

His breathing was labored and his knees were trembling. The concierge knew something, there was no doubt of that, something that was going to cause him distress.

"Had you been married long?"

"Almost twenty years."

"She'd been coming here for the last eighteen years."

His throat was so dry that he could hardly speak. Inwardly, he cursed Sergeant Fernaud and his equivocal manner.

"Did she come often?"

"Not every day, but at least three times a week . . . Surely as her husband, you have a right to be told . . . When they first took the apartment, I thought they were husband and wife. He was one who chose all the furniture, and the rugs and curtains—and I may as well tell you that nothing but the best was good enough for him."

"Has he given up his lease?"

"No. And he still comes occasionally. As far as I can remember, they stayed the whole night on only two occasions. The first time was about three years ago . . ."

Three years ago he had spent a couple of days in Antwerp buying diamonds.

"The second time," she went on, "was only a few months back . . .

"One thing you can be sure of—those two were very much in love. Monsieur Brassier always got here first, and he never came empty-handed, but always brought chocolates or cakes."

He could not believe his ears.

"What name did you say?"

"Monsieur Brassier. He had to use his real name for the lease. I thought at first it wouldn't last long, and that there would be others after her. But no . . . they were as much in love after eighteen years as at the very beginning."

132

"You are talking about Jean-Paul Brassier, are you not?"

"Who else?"

"Did they stay up there long?"

"He usually arrived just before three, and she would be there soon after. Mostly she left between five and six, and she always seemed in a great hurry."

"Who cleaned the apartment?"

"I did. That's how I came to know them so well. . . . Just imagine, the walls of the bedroom are covered in yellow silk . . . there's silk everywhere. Her outdoor clothes were very plain . . . she usually wore a suit or a navy dress . . . but you should have seen the underclothes and housecoats she kept up there!"

He had not the courage to ask her to let him see the apartment. He felt utterly drained. He was more deeply shocked even than by his wife's death.

His wife? Had he really any right to call her that?

This had been no passing fancy, no casual affair lasting a few weeks or months.

For eighteen years, she had been coming regularly to Rue Washington, not to cheap furnished rooms, but to an apartment full of things lovingly chosen for her. And she had kept a stock of clothing there.

When he had returned from visiting his father, she had said, quite casually, as though it were of no great importance:

"I spent the whole of last night with a poor old man who was in dreadful agony. But for me, he would have died alone."

She had lied to him. She had been lying to him for eighteen years. She had not been his wife. If she was anyone's wife, she was Brassier's.

And he, too, had lied about his round of afternoon calls.

133

Did Eveline know? Very likely. She was much too self-centered to suffer from jealousy.

"Thank you, madame."

Somehow he stumbled out into the street. He wandered aimlessly in the direction of the Champs-Élysées. It did not even occur to him to stop for a drink.

He had never really liked Brassier, but now he hated him. Annette was another matter. He could not blame her. It was he who had been at fault. He had not been the right husband for her. He had taken her to be a very simple person, interested in nothing but her charitable work. He had never known her as she really was.

And it was this, one might say, which had caused her death. She had been running. Probably she was a little late. She was in a hurry to get to the Métro. The journey would give her time to calm down, to resume her customary mask of placid serenity.

She had never loved him, only Brassier.

And yet she had gone on living with him. For eighteen years she had kept up the pretense of being his wife.

What was there for him to do? Kill his partner?

He could not see himself buying a revolver, waiting for Brassier to come into the shop, and shooting him there and then, without a word.

What good would it do anyway?

He walked straight past the Métro station. He went on walking. From time to time, his lips moved as though he were talking to himself. He had a cigarette in his mouth, but it had gone out and was stuck to his upper lip.

For twenty years, he had been the happiest man on earth. He had lived in modest style, but married to the woman of his choice and earning his living by the work he loved.

He had often said to Annette:

"You know, I just couldn't be happier. It's almost too much. Sometimes it frightens me."

He had had good reason to be frightened. Not only was Annette dead, but she had always loved someone else. Brassier had attended the funeral. Célerin had barely noticed him. He had been too grief-stricken to notice anyone. But he did recall now that Brassier had been the first to throw a flower into her grave, a single red rose.

Red roses had been Annette's favorite flowers. He could not remember when he had last given her any. It was not in his nature. If he had brought her flowers, she would, if anything, have been a little taken aback.

But surely what mattered was that he loved her?

It had never entered his head that his wife might find him inadequate. It was men like Brassier who were thoughtful in that way. He had had the walls of *their* bedroom covered in yellow silk.

And had he also provided a white satin counterpane, like the one in his house at Saint-Jean-de-Morteau?

Without knowing it, he had walked all the way to Place de la Concorde. What was he to do? Where was he to go?

He was tempted to go home and unburden himself to Nathalie. Had she not always preferred him to Annette? No doubt there were things that had not escaped her shrewd feminine eye.

But it would be cowardly to attempt to shift his burden onto someone else. What had happened had happened, and he had better face up to it by himself.

The truth of the matter was that Annette had died twice over.

He walked with his arms swinging wildly and his

head in the air, heedless as a village idiot. Whenever he bumped into anyone, he looked at them in bewilderment and stammered an incoherent apology.

No doubt they thought him drunk. He had considered getting drunk, but he knew that it would only make things worse, and exacerbate his grief.

He strode along Rue de Rivoli with no conception of where he was, coming to a sudden halt from time to time as some new thought struck him.

He did not have the courage to face his co-workers. He went into a bar, ordered a small bottle of Vichy water, and bought a token for the telephone.

"Hello, Madame Coutance. Is everything all right?"

He was still capable of making polite noises.

"Would you put me on to Daven, please?"

He heard her call him, and then the sound of approaching footsteps.

"Hallo! My dear fellow, aren't you feeling well?"

He was usually the first to arrive in the morning, and he had not spent three days away from work since the founding of the firm.

"Not too good," he murmured.

"Are you in bed?"

"No. There's still something I have to do in town."

"Have you seen a doctor?"

"No."

"You should. By the way, Brassier is here. Do you want to speak to him?"

"No. I just wanted to let you know that I might not be coming in for the next few days."

"May one come and see you?"

"It's very kind of you, but I'd rather not . . ."

"Well, anyway, I hope you'll soon be better."

"Thanks. Good-by."

He went home. Nathalie was cleaning, and all the

windows were open. She looked up from her work, subjected him to a close scrutiny, and switched off the vacuum cleaner.

"You look terrible."

"I feel rotten."

"You've had a shock?"

"God! Yes."

"Go to your bedroom. What you need is rest. When you're in bed, I'll give you something that will make you sleep for a few hours. I'm glad to see that you haven't been drinking."

He gave her a sharp, mistrustful look.

"How did you know I had had a shock?"

"Because you're not the sort of man to get into such a state without good reason."

"You knew?"

"My dear monsieur, I knew . . . and at the same time, I didn't.

"There are things that a woman can't help noticing. When your friends came to the house, the signs were all there. Your wife's eyes were brighter . . . she had more color in her cheeks . . . and glances were exchanged . . ."

"Are we both thinking of the same man?"

"Monsieur Brassier, yes."

"Do you think his wife knew, too?"

"I'm sure of it. She pointedly ignored what was going on under her nose."

"They were in love."

"Yes."

It was very hot in the flat. He took off his jacket.

"Did you go to Rue Washington?"

"I've just come from there . . . How did you know the address?"

"When I heard that she came out of a nearby house

137

before she stepped off the sidewalk, I guessed at once . . . I was afraid that you might come to the same conclusion and go there to investigate."

"They've had an apartment there for eighteen years, and the concierge says it's exquisitely furnished and decorated. If only . . ."

"If only what?"

"If only she had told me."

"She hadn't the heart to shatter your illusions. You were so happy, so trusting . . . you were radiant with happiness."

"That's true. There were times when it frightened me. Maybe I had a presentiment . . ."

"Well, you've just got to put it out of your mind for the present, at least until tomorrow. Do you hold it against her?"

"I don't know. I haven't had time to think . . ."

"You mustn't blame her too much. It's impossible to conquer a feeling as deep and enduring as that. It must have hurt her terribly to have to lie to you, I'm sure it must."

"Do you really think so?"

"She was a woman who did everything to excess."

"What about him?"

"I've never liked him. He's much too sure of himself. But the fact that their relationship lasted eighteen years is a point in his favor. They couldn't have gone on meeting as often as they did if they hadn't genuinely loved one another."

But why? he asked himself again.

Why had it happened to him? Why had it happened to them? But for a stupid accident, he would never have found out. He would just have gone on living his harmless, uneventful life.

138

"According to the concierge, she kept a whole lot of clothes there, elegant underwear and nightgowns."

"I know."

"And how could you possibly have known that?"

"One evening she was dressing while I was in the room. I noticed that she was wearing a brassière that I'd never seen before. She caught me looking at her and blushed. Then she snatched up her dressing gown, put it on, and sent me out to the kitchen for something or other . . . It was quite different from the sort of underwear she wore here . . ."

"I always thought she had very simple tastes."

"Except on Rue Washington . . . and even that, I suppose, was to please Monsieur Brassier . . ."

His face was drained of expression, and all the resilience seemed to have gone out of his body. His gaze flickered aimlessly from the bed to the window, as though he could not think what to do with himself.

"What am I going to say to the children?"

"I'll tell them you're not well, that you haven't properly got over your cold."

"Poor kids. It's no fault of theirs."

"I'm going into the kitchen to get you some fruit juice. In the meantime, you get undressed and into bed."

He did as he was told. He could not imagine what he would have done without her. Walking along the Champs-Élysées and Rue de Rivoli, he had toyed more than once with the idea of suicide.

It would certainly be one way of cutting his losses. An end to brooding. An end to suffering. But there were the children. They had already lost one parent, and lately he and they had become much closer.

He went to the medicine cabinet, intending to take a couple of Annette's sleeping pills.

"No, not those pills," Nathalie said from the doorway. "They're only good for children. I've got some others in my room. There are times when I need them, too . . . We all have our moments of weakness."

She returned with three bluish pills in a saucer.

"Take them all. They won't hurt you."

"I wouldn't mind taking twenty . . ."

"If you did, you'd only be rushed off to the hospital and have a great thick tube pushed down into your stomach . . . that wouldn't be much help, would it?

"Anyway, that's enough talk. Lie down and go to sleep."

She closed the shutters and drew the curtains. A pale, golden twilight pervaded the room.

"Sleep well . . . And don't worry about the children. I'll attend to them."

He lay on his back gazing up at the ceiling, convinced that, in spite of Nathalie's pills, he would not sleep. Nevertheless, within minutes his thoughts became confused. Memories of long-forgotten incidents, mostly from his childhood, floated into his mind. He even rediscovered the taste of the soup his mother used to make.

She had died when he was very young, so that he had scarcely had time to get to know her. Now he could see her face with astonishing clarity.

He could also see the pond at the end of the field. It was overhung with two weeping willows . . . he used to catch frogs there.

It was all very distinct and highly colored, like pictures in a book. He was in the schoolroom, and there was the teacher, with his pointed beard, and the boy with the harelip, and the butcher's daughter, whose braids they all used to pull.

The pictures were fading. He was breathing deeply. He was asleep.

Not only did he sleep until nightfall; he slept right on into the following morning. It was such a good sleep that he wished he could prolong it. He woke up in the middle of a dream. He could not remember what it was about, but he had the feeling he would have liked to know how it ended.

He glanced at the alarm clock. It was half past six.

He got up, put on his dressing gown, and went into the kitchen. Nathalie was sitting at one end of the table, eating her solitary breakfast.

"Ah! So you're awake."

"Good morning, Nathalie. Don't let me disturb you. While you're finishing your breakfast, I'll make myself a cup of coffee."

"Don't you want anything to eat?"

"No."

From now on, he would have to learn to think and behave differently.

"Are the children still sleeping?"

"Jean-Jacques' exams finished yesterday. After all the strain, he was so exhausted that he went to bed without dinner. I thought I'd let him sleep as long as possible. Marlène still has another week of school. I'll go and wake her in a minute."

She was eating thick slices of bread and jam. Suddenly he felt hungry. He put his cup of coffee down on the table, buttered himself a slice of bread, and spread it with red-currant jelly.

This brought back yet another childhood memory.

"That stuff you gave me had an odd effect on me. It brought back memories of things I had completely forgotten."

"Unpleasant memories?"

"No, just incidents from my childhood."

He ate three slices of bread, and got up to pour himself a second cup of coffee.

"I'd better go and wake Marlène. She takes such ages over her bath."

Unlike him, she never got up until the very last minute, and then had to bolt her food and run.

He combed his hair and shaved, then, still in his pajamas and dressing gown, he began prowling around the apartment. Marlène, who was having her breakfast in the dining room, looked up in surprise.

"Better already?"

He bit back the reply that he would never be better, and said instead, in what he hoped was a bantering tone:

"As you see, I never seem able to get really ill, like other people."

"And yet you aren't going to work."

"Not today, possibly not for several days. I need a rest."

"Are you worried about something?"

"A bit."

"I suppose you couldn't tell me about it?"

"I'm afraid not."

She was having boiled eggs for her breakfast, dipping strips of bread into the yolk, just as she had done as a child.

"Jean-Jacques has finished his exams. Did you know?"

"Yes. Does he think he's done well?"

"You know him. He hasn't got a very high opinion of himself. The results won't be out until the twenty-sixth. Until then, he'll do nothing but bite his nails."

Jean-Jacques had never shed the habit of biting his

nails in times of stress. He never talked about himself; nor did he ever mention any friends he might have made at school. And yet he was not altogether an introvert.

"Is he still asleep?"

"He needs his sleep—don't disturb him," interposed Nathalie.

Marlène ran out to get her briefcase, and then planted a wet kiss on her father's forehead.

"See you later. Take care."

"The paper is in the living room. Go sit there and read it while I do your bedroom."

He sat in his leather armchair, which had the patina of old wood. He forced himself to read. A young woman had thrown herself into the Seine, and had been rescued just in time. Four thugs, having committed a number of armed robberies, were today coming up for trial.

It was no good. He was making a tremendous effort, if only to please Nathalie, but he could not help reverting to it.

The pain was unremitting. And, as one probes a sore tooth, he constantly made it worse by picturing, with agonizing clarity, a series of cruelly intimate scenes.

"Now you can go and have your bath."

He stretched out in the hot water, and nearly fell asleep again. Then, slowly, he soaped himself all over. He had nothing to do. He was on holiday, like his son. But, in his case, it was a different kind of holiday.

Reluctantly, he put on a shirt and trousers. He did not want to get fully dressed. He did not want to be tempted to go out. It was an effort even to leave his bedroom.

But he did, and found Jean-Jacques in the kitchen. He was raiding the icebox, as usual.

"Hello, Father."

"Good morning, son."

"Feeling better?"

"Better than yesterday, but still not too good."

"What exactly is the matter?"

"I don't know. A touch of flu perhaps. D you think you've done well in your exams?"

"Let's say I'm not too worried. Anyway, we'll know for sure on the twenty-sixth."

"What are you thinking of doing for the holidays?"

"I won't have as much time as usual this year. I have to be in England at the beginning of September. By the way, I've got a couple of forms for you to sign . . . and you'll have to pay a term's fees in advance. I'm sorry to put you to so much expense . . ."

"Let me have the forms as soon as you can. . . Do you remember that your sister is going to spent a fortnight with a friend at Sables-d'Olonne?"

"Yes. And then she'll be joining you in Porquerolles."

"That's right. I was wondering if you would care to come, too."

"I might, for two or three days. As I shall be away from France for three or four years, I'd like to see a bit of the countryside before I leave. A friend and I thought we might go on a walking tour through some of the more attractive villages. We might hitchhike part of the way."

Célerin made no objection. Anyway, he had not counted on having his son with him during the vacation.

"Have you planned your route?"

"No. We'll go to Brittany first, and take it as it comes."

What use was he to anybody? What use had he ever been?"

It was on his account that Annette had been forced to live a lie. And, knowing her, she must have suffered. But why had neither of them ever asked for a divorce? Because of the children? Or because Eveline would not hear of it?

That, he thought, was probably the explanation. She loved luxury, and money meant a great deal to her. When Brassier had first met her, she had been a young sales girl in the jeweler's shop where he had had his first job.

They had known each other barely two months before they were married.

She was over forty now, and her chances of finding another, equally successful husband were much diminished. Why should she have agreed to a divorce? And Annette had never asked for a divorce either. Had he known that she did not love him, that she loved someone else, he would not have stood in her way. On the contrary, he would have consented to be the guilty party.

Surely it would have been better that way than to discover suddenly, after twenty years, that the whole of those twenty years had been one long deception?

He had opened his heart to her. He had had more faith in her than in all the rest of the world put together. He had never concealed anything from her, not even his most intimate thoughts.

She had listened. She had watched his facial contortions as he shaved. And there had been times when he had wondered why she never talked of herself.

Why should she have done so—to a stranger? For he could no longer pretend to himself that it was other-

145

wise; he had been a stranger to her. A stranger who shared her bed, and made love to her. A stranger who blurted everything out, like a child.

There must have been times when she had longed to find a way of silencing him. But on what pretext? They were married . . . They had two children .

Two children . . . Both were under eighteen. Three times a week, Annette had gone to Rue Washington. Eveline had borne her husband no children.

Was it possible that Jean-Jacques and Marlène . . . ?

He began pacing the room, deeply disturbed, and came close to throwing himself out of the window.

Not half an hour ago, he had believed that at least he still had Jean-Jacques and Marlène.

But were they, in fact, his children? Supposing they were not his, but Brassier's?

He dared not pursue this line of thought to its logical conclusion. It was too appalling to contemplate.

He called Nathalie, and facing her with eyes filled with distress and apprehension, said:

"Don't try to humor me. I want the truth. I've got over the worst. I can take anything now. Does Jean-Jacques look like me?"

"He has a longer face, and his hair is lighter . . ."

"And he has gray eyes, hasn't he . . . blue-gray like Brassier's?"

"A lot of people have blue-gray eyes. You can't really say he looks like him either."

"And Marlène?"

"If she looks like anyone, it's her mother . . . except that she's much taller. I'm always having to let down her dresses and slacks."

"She doesn't look like me at all."

"That doesn't mean a thing. What notion have you got into your head now?"

"He made love to her more often than I did . . . And I've just remembered something. It was when Jean-Jacques was born, and they were still in the clinic. I bent down to kiss the child on the forehead, the child that I believed to be mine, and she put out a hand to stop me. It was a instinctive gesture, so much so that it ought to have aroused my suspicions.

"Later she said, by way of excuse, that it was considered advisable to avoid, as far as possible, bringing newborn babies into close contact with visitors."

"Poor monsieur."

"I am indeed a wretched creature. I wonder if you can imagine what it feels like suddenly to be left with nothing?"

Music drifted into the room. Jean-Jacques was playing a record.

"There's no reason to suppose you're not just imagining it?"

"There's no reason to suppose that I am. Listen to me, Nathalie. I'm at the end of my rope. I'm capable of anything, any madness. . . . Right now, I could choke the life out of Brassier. I wouldn't need a weapon . . . I have the powerful hands of a workingman . . ."

Suddenly he cried out loud:

"No!"

And burst into tears.

7

It was his Gethsemane, and it lasted five days.

"Nathalie! Give me some more of those tablets I had yesterday . . . please."

He had hoped to escape into dreams of childhood, but this time it did not work. It was Annette who haunted his dreams. Annette who, for eighteen years, had been forced to live a lie day in and day out.

All morning, while Nathalie cleaned the apartment, he trailed listlessly from room to room in his dressing gown and slippers.

Time and space had lost all meaning for him. The apartment on Boulevard Beaumarchais seemed as unreal as a stage set, as did the people in the street running, for some incomprehensible reason, to catch their buses.

Meals in the dining room were torture, conscious as he was that the children were watching him. Jean-Jacques was more discreet about it than his sister, but he was unusually subdued, as though he were expecting some new misfortune to befall them.

He himself was incapable of making a joke, of laughing. Sometimes, just to break the silence, he would ask a question, but there was no longer any real communication between them.

"I know you've told me before, but what does your friend's father do for a living? . . . What's her name again?"

"Hortense."

"Do you know what her father's profession is?"

"He's a lawyer . . . He's a big man, and Hortense is the fattest girl in our class . . . You're not listening . . ."

"Of course I am."

"Then repeat what I've just said."

"A lawyer . . ."

"There you are, you see . . . You'd better start pulling yourself together, Father, because if you don't I shall send for the doctor myself."

He had no appetite. He ate almost nothing.

He was always impatient to get back to his bedroom. If it had been possible, he would have slept the whole day.

Most of the time, he just sat in his armchair by the open window. It was very hot. He neither saw nor heard the bustle in the street outside. It had nothing to do with him, enclosed as he now was in a private world of his own.

Nathalie never left him alone for long. She knew that he did not possess a gun, but feared that he might attempt suicide in some other way, probably by throwing himself out of the window. In his present state of mind, anything was possible.

He knew very well why she was keeping a furtive eye on him.

"Don't worry, Nathalie. I won't kill myself . . . I'm past that stage. I did think of it for a time . . . but that's all ancient history . . .'

"I wish you'd get dressed and go for a walk with me."

149

For all the world as if he were a chronic invalid in need of constant supervision!

"I haven't the least desire to go out."

The same thoughts, more or less, going round and round in his head. It was almost as though he took a malicious delight in torturing himself.

The two couples, the Brassiers and the Célerins, had quite often dined together. That must surely have put a severe strain on Annette and her lover?

Eveline, he was convinced, had known what was going on. But, on his account, they had had to watch their step. They had been forced to put on an act. They had avoided looking at one another. He now recalled two occasions on which Annette had addressed Brassier by the familiar *tu* instead of the more formal *vous*, and each time she had stammered out a confused apology:

"You know how it is . . . among old friends . . ."

The memory of it grated on him. It had all been a tissue of lies. Their whole life together had been a lie.

He was sorry now that he had given away his wife's clothes. There were times when he longed to recall the distinctive scent that they would always retain.

He was caught in a trap, and there was no way out. Even the workshop on Rue de Sévigné was owned by Brassier rather than himself.

As to the children . . .

Was there any way of determining who the father was? Would a blood test, for instance, be conclusive?

He was subject to violent changes of mood, alternating between rage and resignation. Those children. It was he who had brought them up. It was he who had tucked them into bed every night. It was he, also, who had taken them out for walks in their baby carriages on Sundays when they were very young.

What did it matter who was their father? They belonged to him now, and Brassier had no conceivable right to take them from him.

There were questions that had to be resolved. To whom had Annette belonged? Not to him. Although he was certain that for the first two years of their marriage she had really tried to love him.

When they had made love, she had made a visible effort to respond. She had been too honest to resort to pretense. Her head would lie listlessly on the pillow. There had been times when she had shed tears.

"You ought not to have married me. I must be frigid, I think; I didn't know . . ."

But he had been confident.

"It will come . . . just relax . . . It will take you by surprise one night, quite suddenly."

And no doubt it had taken her by surprise. Except that it had not happened to her in his arms, but in Brassier's.

How they must both have suffered during vacations, when they were forced apart, unable even to write to one another. He remembered sitting beside her in a deck chair on the beach at Riva-Bella.

He himself had been happy, blissfully happy. He had thought himself the most fortunate of men.

Brassier and he had become close friends and, since they had gone into partnership, had met almost every day. They also visited one another in their homes.

"How is Eveline?"

"Much the same as usual. Lately she's taken to reading quite serious books, but I guess she'll be back with her magazines again before very long. . . . And Annette?"

"She spends most of her time with her 'little old people,' as she calls them. She seems hardly to notice that she's the mother of two children . . ."

He clenched his fists. These things had been said, exactly as he recalled them . . . these and many others.

And now . . .

Nothing. He had reached a dead end. Daven telephoned to find out how he was.

"How are you feeling? We were beginning to get worried about you here."

"I'm feeling a little better."

But more than ever as if he were beating his head against a brick wall!

"I've finished Madame Papin's brooch."

"What brooch?"

"The setting for the emerald she brought in. The one it took you only a few minutes to sketch."

When he had been drunk. There were times when he felt like getting drunk again, but he was afraid of what he might be tempted to do.

"It's been driving me up the wall, assembling that nest of wires and slivers of gold . . . I spent half the night on it. She wants to wear the brooch tonight, to some grand function. Would you like me to bring it over for you to see?"

"No."

"Do you mean to say you've lost interest in it?"

"Yes."

Bitterly, he added, as though to rub salt in the wound:

"Show it to Brassier."

It was an effort to shave in the mornings. He forced himself to do it for the children's sake. Or rather, for the sake of one of his children. Jean-Jacques, with a knapsack on his back, had already gone off on his walking tour with a friend. They had set out dressed like a couple of boy scouts.

"I'll see you in Porquerolle," he had promised.

Marlène was also getting ready to leave.

"Do you mind if I get myself a safari shirt?"

"What's that?"

"It's a sort of lightweight jacket with box pleats on the pockets, and it looks very nice with matching slacks . . ."

They were leaving from Hortense's flat on Place des Vosges. She kissed her father, and clung to him.

"Father, darling, do try and snap out of it . . . you can't go on like this . . ."

He smiled wanly.

"I'll do my best. I promise."

"When I meet you again in Porquerolles in a fortnight, I shall expect to find a father fully restored to life. Do you know what I think?"

"What?"

"I think you should take Nathalie along. It would be a vacation for her, too. It's a shame to leave her alone in the apartment . . . let me tell her . . ."

Obviously she thought he was in need of a nurse.

"Nathalie . . . come here a minute. I've got good news for you . . . Father has decided to take you with him to Porquerolles."

"So that's how he's going to get rid of me!" she said jokingly. "By drowning. He knows I only have to go in the water to sink like a stone."

"What hotel will you be staying at, Father? I don't want to have to chase all over the town looking for you."

"The Hotel des Iles d'Or. I'll call and book an extra room."

"Are you going by car?"

"I haven't decided yet."

Curtains! The children were gone, leaving Nathalie and himself alone in an apartment much too big for them.

"Would it be a bore for you to come to Porquerolles?"

"Far from it! I bet it was Marlène's idea."

"Yes . . . I don't think she liked the idea of my being all on my own there for a fortnight."

For hours at a time he would appear perfectly normal; then suddenly he would be stricken with a severe fit of depression.

Then, one morning, after having shaved and bathed as usual, he went into the living room in his dressing gown, lifted the telephone receiver, and dialed the number of the shop.

"Hello, Madame Coutance . . ."

"You sound a little better today."

"Tell me, is Brassier there?"

"He's just come in."

"I'd like a word with him."

He was very tense inwardly, but when Nathalie glanced at him through the open door, she thought he was looking much better than he had for days.

"Hello."

"Célerin speaking."

"Brassier here."

"I want to talk to you."

Without realizing it, he used the formal *vous*, though they had been on *tu* terms for years.

"When?"

"As soon as possible."

"Are you coming into the shop?"

"No."

"Will you come to my house?"

"No."

154

"Would you like me to come to you? Or could we meet in a restaurant?"

"Too crowded."

"What about the lounge of one of the big hotels?"

That was Brassier all over!

But the plushy lounges of the Georges-Cinq and the Crillon were not for Célerin.

"There's a little bistro on the corner of Place des Vosges and Rue du Pas-de-la-Mule."

"I know where you mean."

"I'll meet you on the terrace. It's usually almost deserted in the early afternoon. Would two o'clock suit you?"

"I'll be there."

Célerin replaced the receiver and stared fixedly into space.

"It feels strange not having the children with us at the table."

He and Nathalie were lunching alone. Nathalie kept glancing at the two empty places. There were, in fact, three empty places, one of which would never again be filled. She had tears in her eyes.

"What are you going to say to him?"

"I don't know."

He was wearing his working suit. Brassier, of course, would be dressed to the nines, as usual, and would surely be driving his new red Jaguar.

Célerin arrived first. As he had anticipated, the terrace was deserted. Even at the bar there were only a few people. It was the slackest time of the day.

"What can I get you, sir?"

"A half bottle of Vichy water."

His heart was pounding so violently that he pressed his hand against it, as if to quiet it down. He had not long to wait before a red car drew up just short of the

155

terrace. Brassier got out, came toward him, and held out his hand.

"No."

Célerin scrutinized his face intently, as though seeking to discover whether he had changed in any way. And indeed he did not seem quite the same man. His self-assurance was in retreat, at least for the time being. His eyes evaded Célerin's.

When the waiter appeared, he ordered a brandy, then called him back:

"Make it a double."

Neither spoke a word. The waiter returned with the brandy, then withdrew into the restaurant. Brassier drank half the brandy, wiped his mouth, and murmured, in a troubled voice:

"You've got it wrong."

"What have I got wrong?"

Mechanically, he had reverted to the familiar *tu*.

"You think I'm a swine."

Célerin said nothing.

"I don't know what you would have done in my place. If I hadn't got married two years before I met Annette, I would have married her."

"But you didn't marry her."

"My wife refused to divorce me. And she's been very careful for the past eighteen years to provide no grounds on which I could divorce her."

"So you and Annette met in secret. You took an apartment and furnished it. You . . ."

Célerin could barely get the words out

"I did all I could to make her happy."

"Because she loved you."

"Yes. She wanted a divorce as much as I did. It wasn't a casual affair. It wasn't a commonplace adultery.

"If it had been, it wouldn't have lasted eighteen years . . ."

"Her death was a tragedy for me as well as for you, only I had to hide my feelings . . ."

"You were the first to throw a flower into her grave."

"It was an instinctive gesture. A red rose . . . red roses were her favorite flowers. There were always some in the apartment."

"Not in our apartment. . ."

Brassier, looking more than a little ashamed, at last found the courage to meet his eyes.

"What are you going to do?" he asked.

"I might ask you the same thing."

"It's out of the question, I suppose, that we should go on working together?"

"Quite out of the question."

Célerin's breathing was labored. He looked longingly at Brassier's glass of brandy.

"The success of the workshop is entirely due to you . . . so, naturally, you will keep it."

"What will you do?"

"Once I let it be known that I'm in the market, I don't doubt I shall get plenty of offers."

The worst was still to come. Célerin wished he could postpone it indefinitely, but the question had to be asked.

"What about the children?"

"I don't know. Annette didn't know either. You and I belong to the same blood group."

"Who told you?"

"Annette looked it up on your medical card. You're group AB. So am I . . ."

"But you made love to her more often than I did."

"Possibly. But that doesn't mean a thing."

"I intend to keep them," said Célerin, with all the firmness he could muster.

"I wouldn't want to take them from you at any rate. Officially, you are their father . . . And, besides, Eveline wouldn't want them."

For the first time since he had known him, Brassier had tears in his eyes.

"Waiter!" he called out. "Another double brandy.

"I haven't come here as your enemy, Georges. I've been wanting to talk to you about it for a long time. . . ."

"Would you have told me the truth?"

"Yes. I knew it would cause you pain, but it would have been worth it to clear all the lies out of the way . . .

"When we used to dine with you, and I saw Jean-Jacques and Marlène . . ."

He was forced to turn away his head. Célerin waited until he had recovered himself.

"Where are they now?"

"Jean-Jacques did brilliantly in his *baccalauréat*. He's gone off around France on a walking tour with a friend."

"And Marlène?"

"She's at Sables-d'Olonne for a fortnight, with a school friend. From there she'll be coming to join me at Porquerolles."

"Will you allow me to see them sometimes?"

"On condition that you say nothing to them about the past."

"I wouldn't be so cruel . . . What are Jean-Jacques' plans for the future?"

"In September he's going to a language school in Cambridge, to improve his English."

"And after that?"

"He hasn't made up his mind yet. He doesn't want to

158

decide anything in a hurry. He takes life very seriously, almost too seriously. He's interested in psychology and sociology, and he would like to take his degree at an American university."

There was a long silence. Georges Célerin looked out at the sunlit square, with its surrounding colonnades, in which children were noisily at play. The houses were all alike—pure Louis Treize in style—and formed a perfect square. Annette and he had brought Jean-Jacques here as a child. Later they had brought Marlène, and, more often than not, it was he who had pushed the baby carriage.

It was a glorious day, one of those days that lovers remember all their lives. There was a couple now, sitting three tables away from them on the terrace, holding hands and looking into each other's eyes as though they would never tire of doing so.

Brassier was the first to regain control of himself.

"When I went to Rue de Sévigné this morning, it was for the last time."

Célerin did not reply. He was still looking out at the Place des Vosges, in particular watching a small boy who was bowling a hoop. It was not often that one saw a child playing with a hoop nowadays.

"I'll instruct my lawyer to draw up the necessary papers."

"I shall want to repay the capital."

"I've been repaid ten times over . . ."

"That makes no difference."

"You'll be hearing from my lawyer. He's Maître Lefort, and his office is on Avenue de Courcelles. Of course, there's nothing I can do legally about the children, but I'll put something in a letter . . ."

"No."

"Why not?"

"Because there are some things that ought not to be put in writing. And besides, there isn't a single drawer in the apartment that I can lock."

"Waiter!"

"You came here at my invitation, so it's for me to pay the bill."

They were both thoroughly ill at ease. Neither wished to be the first to leave.

Finally, Célerin could stand it no longer.

"Good-by," he muttered, not looking at Brassier.

"Good-by, Georges," replied Brassier.

As Célerin walked away along the shaded Rue du Pas-de-la-Mule, he heard the engine of the Jaguar accelerating.